With his star pinned to his shirt and his gunned clipped to his belt, he looked every inch the tough Texas Ranger...except for the infectious smile

Skye walked straight into Sam's arms, and before she knew it, she was dancing as she'd never danced before, feet flying and laughter bubbling from her like an artesian well. One dance led to another and another. She could have danced all night.

Suddenly a woman screamed and a fight broke out at the bar.

Skye froze. Panic hit her like a lightning bolt as the place erupted into pandemonium.

She had to get out!

D0424678

Dear Reader,

For those of you who have been following the Outlaw family books, this is the last of the four brothers and a sister, all named for famous outlaws, following a tradition established by their grandfather. Sam Bass Outlaw's story, *The Texas Ranger*, like Belle's story, *The Rebel*, is set mostly in Wimberley, Texas, a real small town in central Texas known for its guest ranches, artisans and picturesque surroundings.

When I lived in Houston, a talented artist friend used to wax poetic about spending weekends in their river cabin in Wimberley, and other friends used to rave about the charming village, but I'd never been there until we moved to Austin. Cypress Creek and the Blanco River are the stuff of picture postcards, and when the wildflowers bloom it's breathtaking.

Since a big hunk of my heart remains in East Texas with its tall pine trees and the rest of the Outlaw family, we'll revisit Naconiche and the magic of The Twilight Inn Motel as well as meet the newest members of the clan.

In this book, I've also returned to my roots in psychology and hypnosis to deal with some special issues that haunt a heroine I've come to adore, Skye Walker. And I've always been a sucker for tall, dark, handsome Texas Rangers.

Enjoy!

Jan Hudson

The Texas Ranger

Jan Hudson

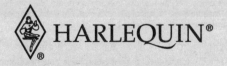

TORONTO • NEW YORK • LONDON
AMSTERDAM • PARIS • SYDNEY • HAMBURG
STOCKHOLM • ATHENS • TOKYO • MILAN • MADRID
PRAGUE • WARSAW • BUDAPEST • AUCKLAND

ISBN-13: 978-0-373-75166-2
ISBN-10:   0-373-75166-4

THE TEXAS RANGER

www.eHarlequin.com

Printed in U.S.A.

ABOUT THE AUTHOR

Jan Hudson, a former college psychology teacher, is a RITA® Award-winning author of thirty books, a crackerjack hypnotist, a dream expert, a blue-ribbon flower arranger and a fairly decent bridge player. Her most memorable experience was riding a camel to visit the Sphinx and climbing the Great Pyramid in Egypt. A native Texan whose ancestors settled in Nacogdoches when Texas was a republic, she loves to write about the variety of colorful characters who populate the Lone Star State, unique individuals who celebrate life with a "howdy" and "y'all come." Jan and her husband currently reside in Austin, and she loves to hear from readers. E-mail her at JanHudsonBooks@gmail.com.

Books by Jan Hudson

HARLEQUIN AMERICAN ROMANCE
1017—THE SHERIFF*
1021—THE JUDGE*
1025—THE COP*
1135—THE REBEL*

SILHOUETTE DESIRE
1035—IN ROARED FLINT
1071—ONE TICKET TO TEXAS
1229—PLAIN JANE'S TEXAN
1425—WILD ABOUT A TEXAN
1432—HER TEXAN TYCOON

*Texas Outlaws

For the heroic Texas Rangers,
past, present and future.

And for the eight great in Travis Country.

Thanks y'all.

Chapter One

When he spotted the blonde across the room, Sam felt as if he'd been hit upside the head with a tire iron. For a minute all he could do was stare at her. And she stared back. He wasn't sure what was going on between them, but he aimed to find out. She was a beauty.

Sam made a beeline through the crowd toward her. The closer he got, the more sure he was that he might have to arrest her. He figured she must have stolen those eyes from heaven. They were big and blue and reeled him in as pretty as if he were a black bass on a twelve-pound line.

"Hello," he said to her, flashing his best smile. "I'm Sam Outlaw, Belle's brother." He figured that the blonde knew Belle since this shindig was given in honor of her buying and becoming publisher of the *Wimberley Star* newspaper.

She smiled back. "I'm Skye Walker, Gabe's sister."

"*Gabe's* sister?" Gabe Burrell was an old friend of Sam's, the host of the party and the guy who was hot for his sister, Belle. "If I'd known that Gabe's little sister looked like you, I'd have been beating down your door. Wonder why he never told me?"

She laughed, a soft chuckle that was both sweet and sensuous. "He told me about you. And so did Belle. You're the youngest of the Outlaw brothers and a Texas Ranger."

"Yes, ma'am. That's me. How about a dance?" It was the best way he could think of to get her into his arms.

Skye's eyebrows lifted as she glanced around the room. "There's no music and no dance floor."

"Darlin', I'm not one to let a little thing like that stop me. There's an empty spot behind the buffet table, and I'll hum." He grabbed her hands and pulled her to him.

A big German shepherd who'd been lying beside her suddenly rose, hackles up. His teeth were bared and a low growl rumbled in his throat.

"Take your hands off me," Skye said.

"Honey, I'm harmless. Honest."

The dog growled again.

Sam dropped his hands.

"Sit, Gus."

The dog sat. But he didn't take his eyes off Sam.

"He yours?" Sam asked.

She nodded. "He's very protective. Excuse his manners. Gus, Sam is a friend."

No stranger to animals, Sam tentatively held out the back of his hand for the dog to sniff. Gus didn't seem interested in getting acquainted. He merely eyed him suspiciously, as if waiting for a reason to take a plug out of his butt.

"May I get you a drink?" he asked.

She held up her wineglass. It was full.

"Okay. How about you get me one?"

Skye looked amused. "What would you like?"

"Anything you want to give me."

She caught the eye of a kid with a tray and motioned for him. She plucked a glass from the tray and handed it to Sam. "Champagne. In honor of Belle's new position. Cheers." She clinked her flute against his.

Sam sipped. "Mmm. The good stuff. Have you raided the food yet? I just got here, and I'm starved."

"Can't have that. Let's find something to take the edge

off." She walked to the spread on the table. He and Gus followed. She handed him a plate and took one for herself.

"Skye, dear, who is this darling man? I swear he's as tall as the door. And just as solid I suspect." The middle-aged woman dressed in purple sparkles flashed a big smile up at him and held out her hand. "I'm Flora Walker, Skye and Gabe's mother. I'm guessing that you must be Sam. I must have missed you when you came in."

"Yes, ma'am. Sam Outlaw. I just got here."

"You look a lot like your daddy," Flora said. "And your brother Cole."

"Yes, ma'am. All the Outlaws look pretty much alike. Mama says we're like peas in a pod." He grinned. "Except for a few things. Cole's the oldest. Frank's the prettiest."

Flora laughed. "And you're full of the devil."

"No, ma'am. That's J.J. I'm the sweetest." He winked.

Flora cocked her head this way and that, studying him for a moment, then she reached up and patted his cheek. "You *are* sweet, dear boy, but you've got a streak of the devil in you, too. I like you, Sam Outlaw. You must let me paint you sometime. Look after Skye. I don't doubt that you can. I'm going to circulate." She fluttered her fingers and waltzed off to a group nearby.

Feeling as if a whirlwind had just picked him up and set him down, Sam watched Flora go. "Fascinating woman."

"Yes, she is," Skye said. "Salmon?"

"Beg pardon?"

"Would you like some salmon?" She'd shoveled some up on a serving spoon.

"Sure." She put some on his plate.

"Aren't you having any?"

She shook her head. "I'm a vegetarian."

"Really? You know, I don't think I've ever met a vegetarian before."

She smiled. "I can't believe that. They may be scarce in Naconiche, but Austin is full of vegetarians."

"Guess we don't eat at the same places. I'm big on barbecue, Tex-Mex and hamburgers. And I don't live in Austin anymore."

"Oh, that's right. Belle said that you've been transferred to San Antonio. Do you like it there?" She piled his plate with roast beef and hers with some pasta salad.

"Haven't seen enough of it yet to tell."

When their plates were full, they found a quiet table in a corner and sat down. Gus tagged along. He didn't look any friendlier.

Trying to make points with the dog, Sam broke off a piece of roast beef and held it out to Gus. He ignored it.

"Is he a vegetarian, too?"

Skye laughed. "No. But he's been trained not to accept food from people."

Sam shrugged. "If our shepherd had been trained like that, I'd have been in a mess growing up. I hated liver, and I always sneaked mine under the table to him."

"I think Belle did, too. He must have been very full on liver day."

"J.J. fed his to the cat. I think Cole and Frank had to eat theirs."

She laughed. "Growing up in a big family must have been fun."

"It had its moments. Do I remember Gabe telling me that you're a veterinarian?"

"I am. I've been in practice for several years."

"Somehow I can't picture you walking around a cow lot in rubber boots."

"I treat cows sometimes, and I've delivered many a calf, but mostly I see small animals in my practice. Cats, dogs, birds. Pets. Do you have a pet?"

"Not since Bounder died a couple of years ago. He was my bird dog. But I could get one. What would you suggest?"

She cocked her head at him the same way her mother had. "Hmm. A toy poodle maybe."

He must have looked horrified because she burst out laughing.

"Bite your tongue, woman. Do I look like the poodle type?"

"Poodles are very smart and very lovable. And quite fearless."

He grinned. "That's me. Smart, lovable and fearless."

"Is that part of the Texas Ranger code?"

"Maybe the smart and fearless. But I don't know of a single Ranger who has a poodle. Wait. I take that back. I think Carson's wife has a poodle. Or is it a Pekinese?"

"The breeds aren't very similar."

"Except that they're both little yappers. Want some more champagne?"

"Thanks, no." Skye glanced toward the door. "Are those your other brothers?"

"Where?" He turned to look over his shoulder. "Well, I'll be. They're here. I thought J.J. and Frank weren't coming because their wives are expecting." He stood. "Come on and meet them."

She hesitated. "Go ahead. I'll meet them later."

"Don't you run off now, darlin'. I'll be right back."

Skye watched him as he strode across the room and slapped backs with his brothers. They did look very much alike. They were all tall, broad-shouldered, dark-haired and quite good-looking. Sam was a charmer, just as Belle had said. And he seemed to have a well-defined sense of himself. He certainly didn't suffer from low self-esteem. Maybe that came from being a Texas Ranger. She'd bet that he didn't lack for female companionship. He surely made her heart skip a beat.

He caught her watching him and winked.

Heat crept up her throat, and she glanced away.

"You okay, Dr. Walker?" Pete asked.

Skye glanced up at Pete, one of four security guards working the party. "I'm fine. Thanks."

He nodded and stepped back to his post, his eyes scanning the crowd.

In a moment, Sam was back. "You look like an orphan sitting there by yourself. Come on and join the party." He pulled her to her feet.

Gus growled again.

"Gus, hush!"

Sam eyed the dog. "Listen, fella, you and I are going to have to have a serious talk."

Gus didn't relent. Skye squatted down and ruffled his scruff. "Gus," she whispered, "you're embarrassing me. Behave yourself. Sam is a good guy. He won't hurt me."

Gus licked her chin.

As she rose, Sam put his hand to her elbow to help her up. "Come meet J.J. and Frank. Did you know that Gabe sent a private jet after them? Their wives hated to miss the party but figured that they could do without the guys for a few hours. Cole's wife Kelly is their doctor, so they're in good hands in case one of them goes into labor."

Sam guided her to where his brothers were talking with Gabe and Belle. Gus pushed his way between them and walked along, too.

Flora had taken Nonie and Wes Outlaw, Sam's parents, under her wing and was escorting them around the room, chatting with this small group and that. Skye wished she was as socially adept as her mother. Even though she knew almost everyone in the room, she was still uncomfortable in the crowd, feeling not only awkward but a little panicky as well.

Gus bumped against her trying to move her apart from Sam, but for some reason she clung to his arm, feeling safer when she could touch him. Odd for her. She was usually wary of strangers.

Skye had already met Cole, the oldest outlaw brother and a former cop who was now taught criminal justice. He'd driven his parents to Wimberley, and they were staying with her family for the weekend. Sam introduced her to his brother Frank, a judge, and to J.J., a sheriff.

"Leave it to you, baby brother, to latch on to the prettiest woman in the room," J.J. said.

"Gee, thanks," Belle said, punching J.J. on the arm.

"Sorry, Madam Publisher, but sisters don't count. Did I hear there was some grub here?"

Frank smiled at Skye. "And leave it to J.J. to find the food. Pardon his manners."

"Skye," Gabe said, "would you show J.J. and Frank to the buffet? I see a new batch of folks arriving. Looks like the mayor."

Frank and J.J. each offered Skye an arm, and they headed to the food with Gus and Sam trailing behind. The dog was careful to stay between Sam and Skye.

What was it with that dog? Sam wondered. Gus didn't seem at all disturbed by Frank and J.J. being around Skye, just him. Sam was a little pissed about it. Dogs and babies always liked him.

Between his family and the rest of the people at the country club party, he didn't get any more time alone with Skye. A couple of elderly ladies, twins from the look of them, cornered him and grilled him for half an hour about the Outlaw family and about being a Texas Ranger. He really didn't mind. Lots of folks were fascinated with both the story of his family's names and occupations as well as everything about the legendary Rangers, but he'd rather have been spending his time with Skye.

"Well," Sam said, "My granddaddy was Judge John Wesley Hardin Outlaw, and he figured it was a political asset to be named for a famous outlaw. He named his boys John Wesley Outlaw, Jr. and Butch Cassidy Outlaw and encouraged them to go into public service. My daddy, who's known as Wes, was sheriff of Naconiche County for years, and Uncle Butch was in the Texas legislature. My daddy just followed the custom in naming his kids."

"And your uncle?"

Sam shook his head. "Died a bachelor."

"We know that Belle is Belle Starr Outlaw and that she was in the FBI," one sister said.

"Yes, ma'am. She's the one who finally bucked tradition when she left the bureau. My brother Cole used to be a homicide detective in Houston, but he teaches criminal justice in college now."

"Cole. That's for…?"

"Cole Younger Outlaw. J.J. is Jesse James Outlaw and he's a sheriff. Frank James Outlaw is a judge, and I'm Sam Bass Outlaw, Texas Ranger."

"How every interesting," one of the ladies said.

"Is it true," the other one asked, "that there are only a hundred Rangers in the entire state?"

"Used to be," Sam told her, "but we've added a few more. There are a hundred and sixteen of us now."

"I don't see your badge," the other one said.

He pulled back his suit coat to show them the distinctive silver star on his shirt.

The first one leaned closer for a look. "Marvelous. Alma, look what it says."

Alma leaned closer, too. Two old ladies reading his chest wasn't Sam's idea of a good time, but his mama had trained him to be polite. He waited until they'd studied his badge before he let his coat fall back into place.

"Oh, there you are, Sam," Flora said, sweeping into their threesome. "Ladies, will you excuse me if I borrow Sam for a minute? There's someone I want him to meet." Without waiting for a reply, she whisked him away as pretty as you please.

"Thank you, ma'am."

Flora tittered. "You looked in pain. Alma and Thelma Culbertson mean well, but they can be a trial sometimes. They adore Belle. She met them in her pottery class."

Flora led him to a corner where Skye was talking to a

sharp-looking dude in an expensive suit. Sam didn't like the way the dude was standing so close to Skye or the way he was looking at her. He noticed that Gus didn't seem to care.

"John," Flora said to the guy, "I'd like for you to meet Sam Outlaw, one of Belle's brothers. Sam, John Oates is the mayor of Wimberley."

The two men shook hands and exchanged a few pleasantries.

Flora took John's arm, and said, "I don't think you've met Belle's other brothers, John. Come along and let me introduce you." She waltzed him away before he had time to protest, leaving Skye and Sam alone.

"Hi, again," Sam said.

"Hi, again, yourself."

"Did your mother just engineer that?"

Skye smiled. "She did. I hope you don't mind."

"Not a bit. I was trying to figure out a way to escape the twins and make it back to you. Sure you don't want to dance?"

She laughed again, and the sound of it reminded him of the wind moving through a stand of pines on a spring day.

"Who's John Oates?"

"He's the mayor."

"I mean besides that."

"He's a building contractor."

"Is he married?"

Skye shook her head. "Divorced. We went to school together. I've known him most of my life. I treat his dog Commander."

"Will you treat my dog?"

"I thought you didn't have a dog."

"I'm going to get one."

Chapter Two

"You sure do seem to be humming a lot these days," Suki, the housekeeper, said as she placed Skye's breakfast on the table.

"Must be the lovely weather."

"Humph. I'd bet my last dime it has more to do with a tall drink of water named Sam Outlaw," Suki said.

Gabe lowered his newspaper. "Something going on that I don't know about?"

"Lots of things going on around here that you don't know about," Suki replied. "You spend more time at Belle's place than you do in your own house. You ought to marry that gal if you ask me."

Skye smiled as Suki stomped from the kitchen. Suki and her husband Ralph had worked for Gabe for years, Suki as housekeeper and Ralph as overseer of the compound, and were more like part of the family than employees. Ralph was a big, easygoing man, but Suki was a tiny thing with flashing black eyes who didn't hesitate to speak her mind about everything. Skye adored them both.

"Yeah," Skye said, "when are you and Belle going to get married?"

"As soon as she says the word."

"And what word is that?"

"Yes." Gabe folded his newspaper. "Don't change the subject, baby sister. What's going on with Sam?"

"Nothing's going on with Sam. I've only seen the man once in my life. At the party." She dug into her cereal. "He seems nice. I liked all of Belle's family."

"So did I. And don't get me wrong, Sam's a great guy, but I don't think he's your type."

A sudden flash of anger jerked her head up. "Really? And exactly what is *my* type?"

"Whoa. I didn't mean to insult you, honey. I just meant that he seems a little rowdier than someone I'd pick for you."

"Define *rowdy*."

The doorbell rang, and Gabe seemed decidedly relieved. "That must be Napoleon."

"Suki will let him in. Define *rowdy*."

"Well, I didn't exactly mean rowdy. Maybe high-spirited would be a better term. He's a rough, tough kind of guy in a rough, tough occupation."

"And you don't think I would appeal to a man like that?"

"Skye, I think you're a lovely woman who would appeal to any man. It's just that you haven't shown any interest in anyone since…well, in a long time."

"It's Carlotta ringing the bell," Suki shouted. "And looks like Napoleon is coming up the drive."

Skye sighed and rose. "I guess you're right, Gabe. Let me go tend to Carlotta." She grabbed a banana, then she and Gus headed for the door.

Carlotta was her banana-loving pal, a llama that nobody wanted any longer and had ended up in their pasture. In a moment of mischief, Skye had taught the smart creature to ring the doorbell. It ceased to be amusing after she started escaping from the pasture frequently and trying to get into the house.

"I thought you said Carlotta was going to quit getting out and pulling them shenanigans when you got those sheep for her to tend," Suki said.

"You'll have to admit she's better nowadays. This is the

first time she's rung the bell in a long time. Napoleon and I will put her back in the pasture."

She stepped out on the porch and patted Carlotta as the llama nuzzled close to Skye and sniffed the banana.

"She get out again?" Napoleon asked.

Napoleon Jones, an ex-tackle from Texas State and a hulking brute of a guy, climbed the steps to the porch. Not only was Napoleon her bodyguard, but he was also her assistant at the clinic. Even as fierce-looking as he was, animals adored him, and he was loving and gentle with every fury and feathered creature she treated. He picked her up every morning, drove her the quarter of a mile to the clinic, and stayed by her side until he dropped her off after seeing the last patient in the evening. He'd been with her since before she opened her practice, and she'd be lost without him.

Carlotta's soft lips nibbled the piece of banana that Skye held out to her, and she and Napoleon easily got her back into the pasture with the two sheep. Skye had gotten the sheep for Carlotta to tend and keep her from being lonely. It had worked until today, and the arrangement would continue to work as long as Skye remembered to give her a bit of attention now and then. And a banana.

As Napoleon drove her over to the clinic in the Jeep, Skye thought about what Gabe had said. Sam might have made her as giddy as a teenager with her first crush, but she couldn't imagine him fitting in with her lifestyle. Sometimes she got so angry and disgusted with herself that she wanted to scream. Maybe she should consider therapy again.

SAM WAS STANDING AT THE SINK shaving when he heard the siren outside his townhouse. He dropped his razor and grabbed his gun as he hurried to the door.

An ambulance had stopped at his elderly neighbor's home. Two EMTs raced for the house while her maid stood on the porch calling, "Hurry! Hurry!"

"What's going on?" Sam asked.

"It's Mrs. Book. I think she's had a stroke." The woman was bug-eyed and wringing her hands.

A small hunk of fur came racing out of Mrs. Book's place, shot between Sam's legs and zipped inside his house.

"Oh, that dog! She'll be the death of me!"

"What can I do to help?"

"Lord, I don't know. They'll be taking Mrs. Book to the hospital, and I need to go along with her. Can you see to Pookie?"

"Sure," Sam said.

In a couple of minutes, the EMTs wheeled out his neighbor, loaded her in the ambulance and took off, siren screaming. The maid slapped a key in Sam's hand, ran to her car and peeled out behind them.

Sam checked to make sure his neighbor's door was locked, then went back inside to finish shaving the other half of his face. Slapping on some aftershave, he walked around calling the dog.

Why in the hell would anybody name a dog Pookie?

He was sorry about Mrs. Book's stroke—if that was the problem. Since he hadn't lived there long, he didn't know any of his neighbors very well, mostly just enough to nod to them. He'd met Mrs. Book when she'd pecked on her window one day as he'd walked by. She'd needed a light bulb changed and wondered if he'd mind doing it. She'd seen his Ranger badge and gun and figured he was safe. Since then he'd done another small favor or two for her, and she'd baked him cookies. Good ones, too. Chocolate chip with pecans.

She didn't have much family except a nephew who never came around. Pookie was her constant companion. The dog was cute, spoiled rotten, and the little rag mop had taken to Sam. Every time he grilled on the patio, she managed to crawl through a little hole in the fence between their places and dance around his feet until he gave her a bite of whatever he was cooking. She was partial to rib eyes.

"Pookie! Where are you?"

Sam heard a faint whimper under his bed and got down to check. He found the dog there, cowed down and shaking like a leaf. "Come on out, girl." He scooped her from her hiding place, held her in the crook of his arm and stroked her. "It's all right, darlin'. I know you're scared. Just calm down."

He could almost hear the dog sigh as she relaxed, and she rooted closer to him.

In a few minutes, Sam set her on his bed. "You stay here. I'll be right back."

He went next door and gathered up Pookie's stuff, including food and bowls, her toys and bed. He even found a small carrying crate and lugged it back to his house as well. He figured he could handle one small dog for a day or two. At least she liked him. Most animals did. Except for Gus.

Thinking about Gus reminded him of Skye. Then, of course, lots of things reminded him of Skye. She'd been in his thoughts a good deal.

He glanced at his watch. *Damn!* He was going to be late. He finished dressing and turned to look for Pookie. He couldn't find her anywhere.

Oh, well, she'd come out sooner or later.

He left out plenty of food and water in the kitchen and left her bed and toys in his bedroom. She'd be fine until he returned.

SAM WAS LATER GETTING HOME than he figured on. And later than Pookie had figured on as well, from what he found on the floor. Honestly, he'd forgotten about the dog, so he didn't scold her. Instead, he let her out the back door and cleaned up the mess without too many cuss words. He'd try to remember to come by home a couple of times during the day tomorrow to let her out.

When he checked on her a few minutes later, the patio area was empty. As he went outside to search for her, he heard whining and scratching. He climbed up and looked over the fence and saw Pookie crying and clawing on Mrs. Book's back door.

He felt sorry for the little thing and went and got her.

"How about you and me going to get a hamburger?" he asked her. "I'm hungry."

She seemed happy enough when she stood in his lap and looked out the window as they went to the fast food place a few blocks away. She hadn't touched the dry food he'd left in her bowl, but she downed a good portion of his second hamburger—except the pickles and onions.

Pookie even whined her way into his bed that night. He could understand that she was confused and probably slept with Mrs. Book.

The next day he called the hospital to check on his neighbor, but the one he'd assumed she'd been sent to didn't have any record of a Mrs. Book. He tried a couple of others with the same result. He couldn't contact the maid; he didn't even know her name. Nor did he know the name of her nephew. Sonny, she'd called him.

Sam was even more concerned when he came home at noon the next day to let Pookie out and saw a van in front of Mrs. Book's house with the name of an auction house on its doors. He walked over and spoke to a man who was there, hoping it might be Sonny.

"I'm doing an inventory for the estate sale," the man said.

"What estate sale?" Sam asked.

"Woman who lived here died. Her nephew said to auction off everything."

That was fast. Disgusted with Mrs. Book's family, he managed to get the nephew's name and phone number. When Sam called Sonny to find out what to do with Pookie, the man said, "I don't give a damn what happens to that dog. Send it to the pound if you don't want it."

Sam slammed down the phone and looked at Pookie, who

sat watching him, her head cocked to one side, an imploring look in her eyes.

Hell, he couldn't have anymore sent her to the pound than he could have sent his own mother.

He called Skye Walker's clinic in Wimberley and made an appointment for Saturday, then he went to the building supply store and bought the stuff to make a doggy door.

WHEN SAM GOT TO WIMBERLEY and stopped at the gate, he wasn't sure he had the right place. Why in the world was there a manned guardhouse? He first thought it might be the entrance to a park or something.

Sam rolled down his window. "I'm looking for the veterinary clinic."

"And your name is?"

"Sam Outlaw. I have an appointment."

The man checked a list. "Yes, sir. I have you here. Go straight down the road and take a right at the Y. You'll run into the clinic." He punched a button and the metal barrier opened.

Must be an upscale place, Sam thought as he drove through. He'd heard of gated communities, but he'd never been to a gated vet's office. He parked in the lot in front of a white Austin stone building with a red tile roof, retrieved Pookie and attached a leash to her collar. When he got to the front door, he was even more mystified. The door was locked. What the devil? Had they closed already?

He rang the doorbell, then knocked.

He waited. And waited. The door opened a crack. "Mr. Outlaw?" a woman asked.

He started to say, "Joe sent me," but, instead of smarting off, he answered with a simple, "That's me."

The door opened wider. "Please come in and have a seat. Dr. Walker will be with you in a moment."

Pookie balked at the threshold, and Sam had to pick her up and carry her inside. She was shaking again.

"It's okay, girl," he said, stroking her. "Dr. Skye's one of the good guys. She won't hurt you." How was it that animals always knew when they were going to the vet? He'd had to drag Pookie from under the bed this morning when he was ready to leave.

He heard voices at an interior door, then it opened and the mayor walked out with his Doberman. Wouldn't you know? The dude glanced at Pookie and smiled. "Cute dog."

"My neighbor's."

"I see," the mayor said. "Sam, isn't it?" He held out his hand.

"Yes." Sam stood and shook hands with him.

A guy roughly the size of a tank followed the mayor out of the interior. He checked the peephole in the front door, then flipped a switch on the wall, unlocked and opened the door for the mayor.

"Good to see you again," the mayor said.

John? Jim? Sam couldn't remember. He only remembered that he didn't much care for his toothy smile.

As soon as the lock clicked into place and the switch was flipped back up, the tank turned to Sam. "I'm Napoleon, Dr. Walker's assistant. Come with me, please."

Sam didn't argue. He was meaner looking than any man he'd ever seen on death row, and, although Sam didn't often meet anyone who made him nervous, the tank put him on guard. This guy didn't look like he'd go down unless you shot him—a bunch of times.

He was led into a room where Skye waited. Gus lay quietly in a corner. Gus raised his head and glared at Sam—or did something that passed for a dog-glare. His lips twitched back over his teeth.

Dressed in a blue smock, Skye stood by a tall examining table, scanned a chart. She glanced up when he entered and smiled. "Well, hello, Sam. What brings you here?"

He held out the dog. "Pookie."

Skye took her, and the dog almost went into ecstasy, wiggling and licking Skye. "Hello, sweetie. How are you?"

Pookie arfed. Twice.

Skye cuddled her close. "Somehow I never figured you for the type who'd choose a Lhasa apso named Pookie."

Sam rolled his eyes. "Me, neither." He told her the story of how he came to be her new owner. "I don't know anything about her. I didn't even know what kind of dog she was until you said. She just looks like a dust mop to me. I don't know about her health or if she's had her shots. She hides under the bed a lot."

Skye checked a tag on her collar. "Here's the number of her vet in San Antonio. Why didn't you call the office and ask?"

Feeling a little dumb, Sam managed to grin. "Never thought of it. Guess I was looking for an excuse to drop over and ask you to lunch."

She laughed, took a cell phone from her pocket and punched in a number. She identified herself and asked for information on Pookie. After a few moments, she hung up and told Sam, "All her shots are in order, and she's a bit overweight but basically healthy. Let me examine her to be sure."

Skye set the dog on her examining table, whispered something to her, and Pookie's wiggling stopped. She stood statue-still while Skye looked her over.

After a few minutes, Skye said, "She's fine, just a little sad about the loss of her mistress. It's to be expected. She likes you."

"I feed her hamburgers and steak."

"Leave off the hamburgers and steak, or she'll be a real roly-poly."

She named a dry food that she recommended for small dogs. "She can have a treat occasionally." She ruffled Pookie's coat. "Show dogs of this breed really do look like dust mops, and they have to be carefully and frequently groomed. Her coat has been kept clipped, and I'd recommend continuing that for her comfort and your convenience. She needs a haircut and grooming now before she starts getting painful mats."

"Where do I get that done?"

Skye glanced at Napoleon. He nodded. "Napoleon will get her fixed up. Every few weeks you can take her to any good groomer near you."

Skye handed Pookie to Napoleon, and the dog went into her wiggling and licking routine again for him. She didn't seem to mind his looks. The man spoke to her softly as they left the room.

"Sam, I think it's very sweet of you to take in Pookie."

He shrugged. "I didn't want to take her to the pound. Do you know of anybody who might like to have her?"

Skye looked concerned. "I don't think it's a good idea to traumatize her further. She's probably best off with you."

Sam nodded. Looked like he now had a dog. "How about joining me for lunch?"

"How about you join me at home instead? You and Pookie. Belle is coming over to go swimming this afternoon."

"I don't have a suit."

"I'm sure one of Gabe's will fit."

"It's a deal." The thought of Skye in a bathing suit had him salivating. He'd bet she was a knockout in a bikini.

"You can have a seat in the waiting room until Napoleon is finished with Pookie," she said. "I have a couple more patients to see yet."

SKYE FELT AS GIDDY AS A CHILD at Christmas. She was sure that Mrs. Westmoreland thought she was nuts because of the way she kept smiling during the account of Puffy's numerous hair balls. And certainly nothing was funny about George Bill's parrot, who had picked out half his feathers, but she could barely keep her mind on her patients. She wanted to break out into song and dance around the examining tables.

Sam Outlaw was here, here in her office. She'd thought about him all week, wondering if she would ever see him again. Gabe had said that Sam wasn't her type, but she had to disagree. Sam was exactly her type. No man that she'd met in years had made her chest tighten and her stomach do back-flips.

She wanted to kiss little Pookie for bringing him to her office. And she could hardly wait to see Sam in a bathing suit. He was sexy enough with all his clothes on. Bare-chested, she'd bet he was a serious stud-muffin.

She giggled as she hung up her smock. Where were all these thoughts and feelings coming from? It was as if all her pent-up desires were rattling their cages and clamoring to get out. She'd have to watch herself or she'd scare the poor man to death.

Holy smoke.

Chapter Three

When Sam pulled himself out of the pool, looked at her and grinned, Skye nearly melted into a little puddle. Even his teeth were perfect—as perfect as his abs. He could have been a model, except he probably thought models were sissies. And maybe they were. Sam was all man for sure, and she hadn't been able to keep her eyes off him since they'd left her office. He was gorgeous, and sexuality oozed from him like honey from a comb. She wanted to run her tongue over his chest to see if he tasted sweet.

Suddenly embarrassed by her thoughts, she forced herself to look away and say something to Belle. But Belle was looking at Gabe as if he were an eclair on a doily and not paying the least bit of attention to Sam and her. Gabe was just as rapt with Belle.

Maybe that's why Skye had gone so goofy over Sam. She was envious of her brother and Belle, and wanted the same thing they had. Boy, had she picked a doozy for her first foray into romance in years. Why couldn't she be attracted to somebody sane and simple? Like John.

But no. John didn't make her heart rev up like a race car.

"Come on in the water," Sam said.

"I don't want to get my hair wet."

"It'll dry. Come on in. Or can't you swim?"

"Of course I can swim. I've got a box full of ribbons somewhere that says I can."

Sam walked toward her, trailing water. "Guess I'll just have to toss you in." He grabbed her.

"No-o-o-o!" she screamed. "Don't!"

He laughed, hauled her up and jumped into the pool with her in his arms.

Gus barked, Gabe yelled and she hit the water in a panic.

When she surfaced, Gus had Sam by the arm, and both Gabe and Belle were in the pool yelling and splashing. Pandemonium.

"Gus! Release!" Skye shouted.

Gus let go of Sam's arm, but Gabe grabbed it. "What the hell are you doing?" He drew back his fist.

"Let go of my brother," Belle yelled at Gabe. "What the hell *are* you doing?"

Gabe stepped back. "Sorry. Skye, are you okay?"

"I'm fine, Gabe. I'm fine. Out, Gus. Sam, are you hurt?"

Sam looked down at his forearm. "I was expecting blood, but he didn't even break the skin."

"Thank, God," Skye said. She heaved herself onto the pool apron and, knees still wobbly, went to talk to Gus, who sat by the chair she'd vacated, looking very pleased with himself. She wasn't sure whether to praise him or scold him. She settled for ruffling his coat. "Sam's a friend, Gus. Get that? A friend."

Why was Gus so wary around Sam? It was as if he really thought Sam would hurt her.

"Are you sure you're okay?" Gabe said.

"I'm sure." She wasn't sure at all, but her brother looked so concerned that she didn't want to make a big deal of it. She hadn't felt comfortable in the water for years. Being in the pool made her feel vulnerable—a feeling she avoided in any way possible.

"Don't be such a mother hen, Gabe," Belle said.

Skye felt awful for more than Gus's attack. She didn't want to be the cause of an argument between her brother and someone she hoped would be her sister-in-law. She stood and pasted a big smile on her face. "Yeah, Gabe. Don't be such a mother hen. Gus, stay."

She forced herself to walk to the diving board, mount it and execute what she hoped was a perfect jackknife into the deep end of the pool. Slicing cleanly into the water felt wonderful. A ton of old memories flooded her, good ones, as she pushed up and broke the surface. She hadn't forgotten how to dive.

Or swim, she thought as she began a slow crawl down the length of the pool. When she got to Sam she stopped.

"I'm really sorry about Gus attacking you. When I screamed, he thought you were hurting me. Is your arm still okay?"

"Not a problem." He smiled.

She returned his smile. "Good." She shoved the heel of her hand through the water and splashed him with a face-full of water. Then she laughed and surfaced-dived, heading away from him.

He grabbed her foot. She kicked furiously at him and popped to the surface, anxiety almost overwhelming her. She fought the dreadful clawing in her chest, fought the urge to cry out.

"Please don't grab me," she said quietly. "I have a thing about being grabbed. It makes me go a little nuts."

"Sorry," Sam said, holding up his hands in surrender. "I didn't know. But I understand. With me it's being tickled. My brothers used to hold me down and do it. J.J. especially. I become a wild man when anybody tickles me in the ribs."

"Tell you what," Skye said. "I won't tickle you if you won't grab me."

"It's a deal. Sorry I upset you and got your hair wet."

"It's okay." She flipped onto her back and sculled along, enjoying the feel of the water against her skin, and, surpris-

ingly, feeling safe with Sam close by. Maybe it was because
he was bigger than life or maybe it was because he was a Texas
Ranger, but he exuded an aura of power and control that was
extremely comforting as he paddled along beside her.

It was a lovely feeling.

For the first time in many years she felt free to relax and
enjoy swimming, an activity that had once been an important
part of her life. For that alone, she wanted to hug Sam.

But there were others reasons, too. She laughed.

"What's funny?"

"Oh, nothing. Everything. Isn't it a beautiful day?"

ONCE SHE GOT INTO THE WATER, Skye hated to get out, but she
was turning into a prune, so she reluctantly dragged herself
from the pool and everybody went inside to change. The guys
were going to grill steaks and veggies while she and Belle
made salad and dressing.

Maria, the cook, and her husband, Manuel, had the
weekend off, and Suki and her husband, Ralph, had gone to
visit her sister for the weekend. Only Flora and the two couples
were around—except for the guards, who were always on the
grounds.

When she came downstairs, Skye found her mother in the
kitchen with Pookie and Tiger, her tiny Yorkshire terrier,
dancing around her feet.

"I just put the icing on a chocolate sheath cake," Flora
said. "Maxine is picking me up any minute."

"Aren't you going to stay for dinner?" Skye asked.

"No, dear. Maxine and Bess and I are driving over to San
Marcos for dinner. It's Bess's birthday. Didn't I tell you?"

"It must have slipped my mind. The cake looks scrumptious."

"Mmm," said Belle as she joined them. "I adore chocolate."
She bent and scooped up Pookie, who had taken an immedi-
ate liking to Belle. "You are such a cutie pie, Pookie. I can't
believe you belong to Sam."

"I'd be willing to part with her if you want her," Sam said as he joined them.

"Sorry. Animals aren't allowed in my townhouse."

Gabe walked in. "Move back here, and you can have all the animals you want."

Belle merely rolled her eyes at him.

The doorbell rang, and Flora said, "That must be Maxine. I'll be going now. I should be back by nine."

"I'll walk you to the door and get the alarm," Gabe said.

Skye kissed her mother's cheek, and Sam followed suit. Flora looked extremely pleased by his gesture.

"Don't you ladies get into any trouble now," Sam said.

Flora laughed and patted his cheek. "I can't make any promises, dear boy."

Gabe and Belle walked out with Flora, leaving Skye and Sam alone in the kitchen with the dogs.

"My mother likes you," Skye said.

"Good. I like her, too. And I like her daughter."

For a moment Skye couldn't make herself look up from the ears of corn she'd taken from the fridge. Then she told herself she was being as silly as a teenager. She smiled. "Do you?"

"Yes, ma'am, I do." He touched her chin with his knuckle.

Gus growled.

Sam sighed and moved his hand. "Need any help with that corn?"

"Sure. We usually grill it in the shucks, but we have to remove the silks."

Sam picked up an ear and skinned back the shuck. "Like that?"

"Exactly. But let me get some newspaper to catch the mess."

"Wonder what happened to Gabe and Belle?"

Skye laughed. "Bet they're making out in the entryway."

"I wouldn't cover that bet."

By the time Gabe and Belle rejoined them, the corn was

ready for the grill. The guys tended to the steaks while Belle and Skye handled the rest of the meal, including skewering an assortment of marinated vegetables for the barbecue.

In no time, their meal was done, and they were sitting around the table enjoying the food they'd prepared.

"I can't believe that you're not eating a single piece of this rib eye," Sam said. "It's fantastic."

"Ugh!" Skye said. "Looks gross to me. Sure you won't have more grilled zucchini?"

"Point taken."

Skye glanced at Gus and smiled. She caught Sam's attention and motioned toward her dog. Pookie was cuddled up next to Gus, sleeping.

"Looks like Gus has a new admirer," Gabe said.

"He's been awfully patient with her nipping and tumbling over him," Belle added.

"With Tiger around, he's used to it," Skye said. "Plus he's around rambunctious animals all the time at the clinic."

"Yes," Sam said. "It's only me he doesn't like."

"I'm really sorry about what happened at the pool today," Skye said.

"No harm done."

After dinner, everybody pitched in to clean up, then Gabe found an old Trivial Pursuit game, and they played until Flora came home.

"I need to get going," Sam said, standing. "I don't want to wear out my welcome."

"Not much chance of that," Gabe said.

"I don't know," Belle said. "He eats a lot."

"Look who's talking."

Belle laughed. "I need to get going myself. A publisher's job is never done, and I have paperwork that I've ignored too long."

Sam scooped up Pookie, and everybody moved toward the front door except Skye. As was her custom, she hung back a bit. Sam hung back with her. "I've really enjoyed the day. Could we get together next weekend?"

"Sure," Skye said, her anticipation almost palpable. "I'm almost always here or at the clinic."

"I'll give you a call."

Skye wanted to touch him, to brush her fingers over the rough stubble beginning to show on his face, but she settled for stroking Pookie. "I enjoyed the day, too. Good night."

ON WEDNESDAY MORNING, not too long after he arrived at work, Sam's lieutenant, Heck Pruitt, called him into his office. He had a fat stack of files on his desk.

"Have a seat, Sam," Heck said. "I wanted to talk to you about this case that's been referred to us. Rather, it's a series of cases. Didn't I hear you say that you and Gabe Burrell over in Wimberley are friends?"

"That's right. We're fishing buddies, and he's my insurance agent. I expect that he might become my brother-in-law one day soon."

"Oh?" Heck raised his eyebrows. "Do you know his sister?"

"Skye? Sure do. She's my…veterinarian. Why?"

"Do you know about what happened to her some years back?"

Puzzled, Sam said, "I guess not. Was she involved in a crime?"

"She was a victim, one of several victims of a kidnapper, but she was the only one who lived. Remember the coed kidnappings?"

"Oh, my God. The papers were full of it for months. That was Skye? Gabe's never mentioned a word about it to me."

"Take these files and read over them," Heck said. "We have to decide if we can find any reason to reopen the case. It's been stone cold for a long time. If we could get some help from Skye Walker, it could make all the difference."

"Skye's a really nice woman," Sam said. "I'm sure she'll be glad to help any way she can."

"Maybe. Maybe not. Read the files first, then we'll talk some more."

Chapter Four

Sam read through the files that covered a period beginning ten years before and became more concerned as he read. In each case, a young woman had been kidnapped from a university in Texas and her family contacted for ransom money. The money had been paid in every case but one, the third abduction, where a girl had been taken from Rice University in Houston. She'd been on scholarship, and her mother couldn't afford to pay. Coeds, from freshmen to grad students, had been taken from seven major schools: SMU in Dallas, Rice in Houston, University of Texas in Austin, Stephen F. Austin in Nacogdoches, Baylor in Waco, North Texas in Denton and, finally, Texas A&M in College Station. All except Pamela Fairchild, the junior at Rice, were from well-to-do families. None were ever seen again. Except one.

Skye Walker. The seventh case.

According to the file, Skye had left that morning for a run with her dog. When she didn't return, her roommate became concerned and went looking for her. She'd found the dog, a German shepherd, unconscious from a tranquilizer dart. She'd called the police. Later that day, Gabe had been contacted by phone and instructed to pay a ransom for Skye's return. An FBI comparison determined that the calls and ransom procedures were the same as in the previous coed kidnappings.

Gabe had paid the ransom, but Skye wasn't returned as promised.

The next day her dog had somehow located her and attracted attention by digging and barking. Skye had been found in a plywood box in a shallow grave in a secluded area about a mile from where she'd been abducted.

"My God!" Buried alive. Sam rubbed his hand over his face and swung his chair to face the window. She must have died a thousand deaths in that box. No wonder the security around her was so tight. And they'd never caught the bastard. He was still out there somewhere. Sam wondered if he'd moved to another part of the country to keep up his abductions. Of course he'd netted a fair amount of money. Maybe he'd just retired to Mexico.

He turned around and went back to his reading.

Skye had been dehydrated, severely traumatized and hoarse from screaming when they'd found her. Her fingers had been bloody from trying to escape. And she hadn't been able to remember a thing about her abductor. She'd had total amnesia for the incident, but had worked with psychologists and hypnotists trying to remember.

Nothing.

Of course her abductor hadn't known that she couldn't remember. Sam figured that when had news hit about Skye's recovery, the perp had made tracks.

Bastard. Sorry bastard.

Without information from her, the cases had gone nowhere. He gathered up the files and went into Heck's office.

"Well, what do you think?" his lieutenant asked.

"I think the chances of ever finding the guy who did this are pretty slim unless Skye gives us something to go on. Looks like every lead at the time was exhausted."

"I agree. I'd like for you to talk to Skye Walker again and see if you can come up with anything that would warrant us reopening these cases. She and her brother were cooperative at first, but they later pulled back, and he's been very protective of her."

"I'm not surprised," Sam said. "If it had happened to my sister, I'd do the same. Sure, I'll talk to her. But I'll check with Gabe first. I'll call him now."

Sam caught Gabe at his office.

Gabe was guarded when Sam brought up the subject of the coed kidnappings and his unit's interest in reopening the case.

"Sam, Skye can't remember the man. The last thing she remembers is leaving her apartment that morning. She was in therapy for years afterward, and she's still traumatized over what happened to her. Her life is workable now, and I don't want to rock the boat. You can't imagine what it was like."

"I've just read the case files. It blew me away that she managed to live through it. Seems to me it might help her if we could reopen the case and nab this guy. Do you mind if I ask her?"

"Let me talk to her first," Gabe said. "I'll get back to you tonight."

SKYE'S FIRST REACTION WAS SHOCK, then anger. Was this the reason that Sam had been so interested in her? Was she simply an interesting bug under a microscope and a means for him to become big dog by solving an unsolvable old crime? "So much for my sex appeal," she muttered.

"Whoa," Gabe said as they sat alone in his study after dinner. "I hope you're not thinking that Sam's only interest in you is because you were a victim."

"Sure sounds that way."

"Skye, he didn't even know about your abduction until this morning."

"And you believe that?"

"Of course I believe it. Sam's an honorable man. And, from the looks of him last Saturday, one who's interested in getting to know you better in lots of ways. If you don't want to talk to him, just say the word, and I'll tell him. He'll respect that. But I should warn you, if it's not Sam, it may be another ranger from his unit. I gather that the team has been asked to review the series of abductions for further investigation. It's what they do—reinvestigate cold cases. Need some time to think about it?"

Skye didn't answer right away. She looked down at her hands, fingers laced and gripped in her lap. Tension sent every muscle in her body into its knotted mode. Was this any way to live? Locked in, a bodyguard at her side, jumping at the least little thing? For the longest time, all she wanted to be was safe. All she wanted to do was forget. But she couldn't completely forget. She had a feeling that the nightmares she'd been having were repressed memories trying to surface.

And they scared her.

Terrified her.

But living the rest of her life in limbo was just as terrifying. And knowing that Gabe deserved to be out from under the responsibility of keeping her safe weighed heavily on her thoughts. She was a drag on his happiness, his and Belle's. She knew that. Security had become a prison of her own making.

A prison? Maybe so. But was she ready to leave its safety?

She didn't know. But she knew that talking with Sam could be the beginning of a monumental change in her life. He would want to drag it all out. Every last bit. Even the parts she had buried so deeply that not even she knew what terrible things were there. No psychologist, no hypnotist had been able to reach it. It must be horrible.

Skye took a deep breath and looked up at her brother. "Tell him that I'll talk to him tomorrow afternoon. Does he know that I have amnesia for the…event?"

Gabe nodded. "He knows."

She left, went to her room and threw up.

SKYE DIDN'T SLEEP MUCH THAT night. Gabe had to come into her room twice to awaken her from a nightmare. An intercom connected her bedroom to his, and her screaming or Gus's barking always brought him to soothe her back to sleep.

She'd been distracted at yoga class with Belle and at lunch later with Belle and Gabe.

"You don't have to do this," Gabe said as they drove home from town.

"Yes, I do. It's time."

She'd gone up to her sitting room to read, but she was still on the same page a half hour later when there was a knock on her door.

Startled, her heart pounding, she said, "Yes?"

"Skye, it's me. Sam."

Rising quickly, her book fell from her lap, knocking over a vase of gerbera daisies on the coffee table. Water went everywhere. "Oh, damn!"

Another knock came.

"Just a minute!" she yelled and ran for a towel from the bathroom.

Unsettled, Gus ran with her, barking.

Sam knocked again. "Skye, are you okay?"

"I'm fine," she called. "Just a minute. Gus, sit!"

Gus sat, but he obviously didn't like it and snarled at the door while she mopped up water from the table and tried to blot it up from the floor. "Oh, double damn!" She stuck the flowers back into the narrow-necked vase and tried to replace it on the table, but without the water to balance the weight, it kept listing, and she'd have to grab it to keep it from falling over.

Finally, holding the vase, she stomped to the door and swung it open.

Sam grinned and glanced at the flowers. "For me?"

"I—I had an accident. Let me put some water in these.

Have a seat." She gestured to the couch and chairs in her sitting room. "I'll be right back."

By the time she'd returned with the vase, Sam was sitting on the couch, his white hat in his hand. Gus still sat where she'd ordered, but he made low rumblings in his throat as he eyed Sam. Sam stood, and Gus's ears went back.

"Gus, down. Stay. Quiet."

Gus followed her commands, but he kept an eye on Sam. What was it with that dog and Sam?

"Sorry that Gus is being rude, Sam. I got upset over this blasted vase of flowers, and I suppose that he associated my agitation with you."

"No problem." Sam laid his hat on the coffee table. "Skye—"

"May I get you some coffee? Or a Coke?"

"No, thanks. Skye—"

"I'll bet that there's some juice in the fridge if you'd rather have that."

"I'm fine, thanks."

She jumped to her feet. "I think I'll have something." She hurried to the mini-fridge disguised as a small chest and opened it. Grabbing a bottle of orange juice, she said, "Sure you don't want something?"

"I'm sure."

She opened the bottle and took a couple of swigs. Her hands shook, and she dribbled juice down the front of her blouse. "Triple damn! Excuse me." She hurried to the bathroom again and blotted at the juice stains. They still showed on her white shirt. Quickly she changed her shirt and left the juice in the bathroom.

"Sorry," she said when she returned. "I'm such a klutz sometimes."

"I think you're nervous."

She took a deep breath. "I think you're right."

"I won't bite. I promise." He grinned.

How could she resist that expression? It was the epitome of the term *boyish grin*. She smiled. "I know you won't."

"Do you mind if I take notes and record our conversation?"

"No, but you won't have much. I don't remember anything."

"Nothing?"

She shook her head.

Sam set a small tape recorder on the table and took a pad and pen from his pocket. "What was the date?"

"May 8. Six years ago."

"See. You remembered that."

She made herself take deep breaths and unlace her cramped fingers. "The last clear memory that I have is waving to my neighbor as Kaiser and I began our run."

"What was the neighbor's name?"

"Mrs. Howard, I think. I'm sure it's in the police report. She said she was baking some gingerbread and that I should stop by for some after my run. I love gingerbread, and I can remember the smell of it."

"So you can't remember the man who grabbed you?"

She shook her head. "Not really. Sometimes I think I see his face in my dreams, but when I wake up, it's gone."

"Do you remember any of your time…before you were rescued?"

"I have vague memories of fear and panic, that terrible fear of being trapped and unable to escape. It's not clear. Nothing is clear except the feelings. They've never left me. If I could remember anything helpful, Sam, I'd tell you. God knows, I'd like to know that the man responsible is locked away behind bars. He needs to pay for all the horror he inflicted on the other women he abducted. The ones who didn't escape. If it hadn't been for Kaiser…"

"Kaiser?"

"Kaiser was Gus's sire. Somehow he managed to track

me. I remember hearing him bark, and I screamed and screamed. And I can remember suddenly seeing the sky. Then nothing until later in my hospital room. Gabe and Mother were there. Big blocks of time are gone. The doctors say it's not uncommon and that I may never remember."

"Did you see a therapist afterward?"

"For years. Two different ones."

"Did you ever try hypnosis?"

Skye nodded. "Early on. It didn't help."

"Would you be willing to try again now?"

She hesitated and swallowed down the bile building in her throat. "I would need to think about it. It's not that I don't want to be helpful. It's simply that I became extremely agitated during the hypnosis and I had terrible nightmares afterward."

"I'm certainly no expert in the area, but I understand that we can secure one of the best in the state who has helped in numerous cases."

"But any information that I might give you while under hypnosis isn't admissible in court, is it?"

Sam frowned. "I'm not sure about that. But I do know that right now we have absolutely no leads at all. Any information you could give us would be better than what we have now. Maybe we could build a case without your testimony. Let me ask you something. Do you remember anybody hanging around your apartment before that morning? This guy had to have been watching you."

She shook her head. "Sorry, I don't."

Sam asked her several other questions, and she answered as best she could, but mostly she was a blank. Her head began to pound. She hadn't had a migraine in a while, but she could feel one coming on.

"Sam, I'm sorry, but I don't think that I can talk about it anymore. I'm getting a splitting headache."

He closed his notebook and turned off the recorder. "I understand. I'll leave now. Maybe we can get together this weekend."

"I don't think I'll have any more to tell you."

"I wasn't talking about the case. I meant maybe we could go out or something."

That should have pleased her, but the pain in her head took all her attention. "Call me," she said, and fled to her bedroom for medication.

SAM TALKED WITH GABE for a while about Skye's kidnapping, but he didn't have anything to add that wasn't in the reports he'd read. Except recounting the horror of it.

"Was Skye able to tell you anything helpful?" Gabe asked.

"Not really. She was nervous as a cat, and just talking about it gave her a bad headache."

"A migraine. Damn. It'll lay her low for several hours. She hasn't had one in a while."

"Man, I'm sorry about that. But I had to talk to her."

Gabe shrugged. "I'm not blaming you for doing your job."

After Sam left, he headed downtown to see Belle's office. He'd been promising her that he'd drop by sometime. Wimberley was a pretty little town full of old rednecks, an artsy crowd plus a new influx of retirees and folks attracted to the charm of a small town and the bucks to be made with the booming tourist trade.

He followed Ranch Road 12 toward the square, passing over the bridge where Cypress Creek had smoothed the limestone boulders along its bumpy path. Not that he could see anything square about the square. There was a crooked Y in the road and a couple of streets off to one side with a bunch of shops and restaurants painted different colors. His mother would call the town picturesque.

He found the *Wimberley Star* office down one of the side streets and parked out front. Belle liked it here. Mostly he figured that Belle liked it here because Gabe was here.

Gabe was a good guy.

And Skye…

Skye was spectacular. She didn't deserve what had happened to her. Sam wasn't exactly sure how he was going to do it, but somehow, some way, he was going to track down the bastard who had screwed up her life and put him behind bars.

Chapter Five

On Friday morning, Skye was just finishing up a surgery when Napoleon said, "You have a phone call on line two. That Ranger man. You want to call him back?"

"No, I'll take it. I'm done here. Would you put Buster back in his cage?"

Napoleon nodded and gently lifted the cat while she stripped off her gloves and picked up the phone.

"Hi, Sam. This is Skye."

"Hope I didn't get you at a bad time."

"No. I have a minute, but I have to tell you that I haven't made a decision yet."

"I'm not pressuring you," Sam said. "And the call isn't business. It's personal. Belle was telling me that she and Gabe often go dancing at a place called Fancy's on Friday nights. I was wondering if you might like to go tonight. With me. And with Gabe and Belle."

"Oh, Sam, I don't know. It might be fun, but I haven't been dancing since— Well, I haven't been in a long time. I doubt if I remember how to two-step. I don't go out much."

"Well, darlin', it's time you started. And I'm a two-steppin' terror. It'll all come back to you. I'll be there about seven. Maybe we can grab a bite somewhere. Listen, I gotta run. See you tonight."

He hung up before she could protest further. She couldn't go out dancing. There would be a mob of people there. Just the thought of going out into such a setting was enough to make her break out in hives. It had taken her months to be comfortable going to church surrounded by her whole family and sitting in the balcony with Gus and two bodyguards. She could handle lunch with Gabe and Gus at a small, familiar café, and she'd come a long way in going to yoga class with Belle and Gus, but *dancing* at Fancy's? A zoo would be calm and quiet compared to that place on Friday night. No way. She'd have to call him back and cancel.

But she didn't know where to call, and she got busy. The next thing she knew it was noon.

Everybody usually congregated at the house for lunch, even Napoleon, who could eat more than any three men, and there was always a big spread, plenty for drop-ins. Belle had picked up Flora from the Firefly, an art gallery that displayed her soul paintings, and joined them for the meal.

When Skye was about halfway through her salad, her mother said, "I'm definitely buying the Firefly. Mason and I are signing the papers this afternoon, and I'm taking over on Monday."

"Fantastic!" Belle said.

"Mom," Gabe said, "are you sure that's not too much for you? Running an art gallery is demanding."

"Oh, fiddle, there's nothing demanding about it. Mostly I just sit there and paint until someone wanders in. I'm hiring Grace Winslet to work part time, including some weekends, and her daughter is going to help out, too. She's a junior over at Texas State and needs a job. Misty, her name is. Very responsible girl."

Skye said, "Mom, I think you should do what makes you happy."

"This makes me very happy. I love being downtown in the thick of things, and I really enjoy people coming in just to watch me paint. It's good company. I'm not cut out for painting in a lonely garret."

"I'm excited for you," Skye said. "It sounds like a wonderful new venture, Mom. And by the way, Belle," she added, trying for a casual tone. "Sam called this morning. He asked me to go dancing tonight at Fancy's."

Everybody stopped eating. Except Napoleon.

Belle's eyebrows went up. "Did he now? And what did you say?"

"He didn't really give me time to say anything before he hung up. But I don't see how I can go."

"Sounds like a fine idea to me," Suki said as she passed the potatoes to Napoleon.

"Oh, Skye," Flora said, "I think it would be great fun for you. And a wonderful experience. Why, Belle and Gabe will be there. And Sam certainly can protect you with that gun he wears on his belt."

"And I'll take my gun if you want," Belle said. "Not that there's any need of it. I'm sure you know almost everybody there."

"I don't want you to do anything that makes you uncomfortable, Skye," her brother said. "Don't let anybody pressure you into something that you're not ready for."

Belle rolled her eyes. "We're not talking about going into a war zone in a foreign country. It's downtown Wimberley, for gosh sakes. What are you going to wear, Skye?"

"I hadn't thought about it. Do you think the place will mind if I bring Gus?"

"I'm sure they won't," Flora said. "Gabe, why don't you call to be sure? And for good measure, perhaps a couple of the guards could be there, too."

Gabe hesitated for a moment. "Skye, if you'd like to try it, I'll make the arrangements."

Inside, her stomach felt as if she'd swallowed a handful of marbles, but she fought to contain her nervousness and managed a smile. "Maybe I could try it for an hour."

Gabe nodded. "I'll take care of things."

WHEN SAM OPENED THE DOOR to his place, Pookie met him, dancing around his feet and yapping until he picked her up. "How's it going, girl? You keep the burglars out?"

She wiggled and licked his face.

"Not on the mouth, Pookie. Not on the mouth." He held her away, then put her down, but she wasn't deterred. Excited, she circled his feet as he made his way to his bedroom, where he dumped a handful of junk mail into the trash.

The light was flashing on his answering machine. He hoped it wasn't Skye canceling their date tonight.

It wasn't Skye's voice he heard on the playback. It was Gabe's. And from all the arrangements he'd made, you'd think they were preparing for a presidential visit instead of going dancing at a local honky-tonk.

"And you've been invited," Sam said to the dog. "Want to go play with Tiger tonight?"

Pookie barked. She seemed to be ready and willing.

Sam took a quick shower, put on his dancing duds and pinned his star on his shirt. He clipped his gun on his belt and scooped up the dog. "Let's boogie."

SKYE CHANGED CLOTHES four times. And her hair wouldn't do anything right, even though the short cut had always suited her fine. She could step out of the shower, towel it dry, finger comb it and be ready to go. Wouldn't you know that her mop had picked that evening to act up? It looked as if she'd stuck her finger in the proverbial light socket—except the left side, which was flattened to her head.

She'd finally settled on a pink patterned tee with a sprinkle of sequins that her mother had given her for her birthday last year and a comfortable pair of jeans and boots. But her hair! How could she go anywhere looking the way she did?

There was a tap on her door. "Skye?" her mother said. "Are you dressed? Sam's here."

She flung open the door. "I can't go. My hair is a mess. Just look at it."

"Calm down, dear. I think your hair looks cute, except for right here." She patted the left side. "Do you have any gel?"

"Heavens, no."

"I'll be right back." Her mother hustled out, stopping long enough to shout downstairs, "We'll be down in a minute."

Skye felt so foolish—like a teenager on her first date. The idea of going out into a mob of strangers was nerve-racking enough. Add the fluster of trying to dress for the evening, and her anxiety level was off the chart. Why had she ever agreed to such a thing?

That was easy. Sam Outlaw. The thought of him made her toes tingle.

She could do this. She could.

Her mother returned with a basket of stuff. "I thought you went after some gel."

"I did," Flora said. "Sit down here."

Skye sat down at the desk in her sitting room, and her mother squirted and sprayed gunk on her hair and picked and poked at it.

"Finished?" Skye asked.

"Not quite. Wait a minute until that dries. It looks really cute."

"Let me see." Skye started to rise, but Flora put a hand on her shoulder.

"Be patient for a moment, dear. Close your eyes."

She felt a brush across her lids. "What are you doing? That's not eye shadow, is it? I don't wear eye shadow." She felt another brush across her cheeks. "Or blush. I don't want to look like a clown."

"It's just a touch, dear. Close your eyes again, please. And don't wiggle so."

"Is that mascara? Good Lord, I'll look like a raccoon."

Flora tittered. "No you won't. Open your mouth just a tad.

And don't get upset, it's only pink lip gloss. There. Now you can look."

Skye hurried to the bathroom mirror, expecting to see something akin to a hooker, but she was shocked. Her hair looked kind of spikey and not too bad, and the makeup was subtle and very flattering. When she rejoined Flora, she bent and kissed her cheek. "Thanks, Mom."

Flora beamed. "You're welcome, dear. You look lovely. Here, slip this in your pocket." She held out a tube of lip gloss.

The final stamp of approval came when she went downstairs and into the den, where Sam had joined Gabe for a drink.

He stood and a smile spread over his face as he looked at her. "Wow," he said.

Her stomach settled, and a warm glow stole over her. Wow, indeed. It was Sam who was wow material. He wore a starched white shirt with the cuffs rolled back and low-slung jeans that emphasized his long waist and slim hips. His shoulders seemed enormous. With his star pinned to his shirt and his gun clipped to his belt, he looked every inch the tough Texas Ranger. Until he smiled in that infectious way he had.

"Ready to go boot-scootin'?" he asked, sidling toward her with a playful shake of his hips.

She chucked. "You'll have to feed me first."

"I'll get the car," Gabe said. "We'll pick up Belle on the way."

DINNER WAS GREAT. They ate at a small Mexican restaurant where she had eaten many times, so there wasn't a problem. Except to wonder where Sam put all those enchiladas.

Walking across the street to Fancy's was a different story. It was night, and cars were parked everywhere, casting hulking shadows and providing hiding places for God knew who. That terrible feeling of vulnerability stole over Skye. Halfway there her knees began to wobble, and she felt a familiar prickly, sweaty feeling in her scalp. She heard the band playing and several "yee-haws" coming from the place, and her knees shook worse. A big lump rose in her throat and she tried to swallow it back down. She could do this. She could. Dammit, she could!

She took a deep breath and lifted her chin.

"Doing okay?" Sam asked softly.

She smiled. "Doing fine."

He offered his hand, and she grabbed it like a lifeline, lacing her fingers through his. The strength she felt from touching him steadied her and she calmed down.

But the calm was temporary. The moment Gabe opened the door, music and crowd noise assaulted them. The place was a mob scene. She tensed, aching to run like crazy.

Before she could bolt, Sam put his arm around her, drew her close and said in her ear, "I've got you."

Gus pushed between them, but Sam didn't let go of her shoulders.

They skirted the dance floor and headed for a table in the corner. Pete and one of the other guards from the compound rose from where they'd been sitting as place holders and turned the table over to the two couples.

When they were seated, Skye looked around and saw several people she knew, who spoke and waved. Sally Olds, her hairdresser, who was in her yoga class, sat at the next table with her husband, Tim.

It seemed as if there were almost no strangers there. Her anxiety level began to slack off.

Sam stood and offered his hand. "Let's dance."

"To *that?*" The band played a fast swing. "I don't think I could keep up."

Sam grinned. "Sure you can. Let's show these folks how it's done."

No way could she resist that grin. Against her better

judgment, she took his hand and stood. Sam led her to the dance floor, then looked down and laughed. "Gus, are you going to lead or am I?"

Gus had followed them onto the floor, and most of the other people were laughing and pointing.

Skye shrugged her shoulders and grinned. "Sorry about that. Give me a minute." She led Gus back to her chair and whispered for him to stay.

He whimpered when she walked away, but he didn't move.

She walked straight into Sam's arms, and, before she knew it, she was dancing like she'd never danced before, feet flying and laughter bubbling from her like an artesian well. One dance led to another. And another. She could have danced all night, but her breath gave out.

"Woman," Sam said, "I thought you said you didn't remember how to dance. You've worn me slap out. Let's take a break before I die from thirst. How about a beer?"

"Sure, I'll have whatever you're having. Along with some water." Skye raked her hand through her damp hair while Sam rustled up their drinks. She glanced over at Pete, who winked at her and grinned. She winked back at him.

"Having fun?" Belle asked.

"I'm having a great time," Skye said. "Sam's a fabulous dancer, the best one here."

"Oh, I don't know," Belle said. "Your brother's no slouch."

"Thanks for that," Gabe said. "How about a dance with me, little sister?"

"Sure, big brother. Just as soon as I get something to drink. I'm dry."

On cue, Sam returned with two beers and a glass of water. Skye went for the water first, then joined Gabe for a waltz.

Gabe was a good dancer. They moved well together— after all, hadn't he taught her? But dancing with her brother wasn't the same as dancing with Sam. He didn't leave her breathless.

Sam must have read her mind because he tapped Gabe on his shoulder. "I'm cutting in. Get your own girl."

Just as Sam took her into his arms, the drummer did a loud riff, and the band started a fast down and dirty number. Sam stomped his feet, let out a "yee-haw" and twirled her out, then back against him and started two-stepping at a fast clip around the floor. She managed to keep up and laughed for the sheer joy of what she felt. She couldn't remember having so much fun in years.

Suddenly, a woman screamed, and a fight broke out to their right.

Skye froze. Panic hit her like a lightning bolt. Beer bottles went flying, another woman screamed, and the place erupted into pandemonium.

Chapter Six

Sam could read the stark terror on Skye's face, and he pulled her against him. "I've got you. Shhh. Nothing's going to hurt you." What a hell of a time for a bar fight. "It's okay, Skye. It's okay."

She trembled in his arms as Gabe and the two guards closed ranks around them. Even Gus jumped in, the stupid dog barking and grabbing Sam's pant leg.

"Let's get out of here," Gabe yelled over the noise. "Pete, you and Ox clear the way to the exit over there."

"I've got your back," Belle yelled. "Go! Go!" It seemed his sister hadn't forgotten her training as an FBI agent.

Sam swung Skye into his arms. "I've got her." He took off behind the guards, but the damned dog was giving him fits. "Get Gus off me!"

"Gus! Release!" Gabe commanded.

Gus hung on, growling and ripping Sam's jeans as the man dragged the dog along on his way to the exit. By the time they got to the door, the fight had stopped, and they were the show. Everybody had stopped deadstill to stare at them. Sam was mad enough to spit railroad spikes. He wanted to turn the air blue and knock some heads together for scaring the life out of Skye.

"Gabe, get the car," Belle said.

Gabe didn't argue. He ran for the car and was back, zooming to a stop in seconds. Belle grabbed Gus's collar. "Skye, you're going to have to call off Gus."

Skye managed a shaky command to the dog, which, thank God, he obeyed. Belle snatched open the back door; Sam climbed in and held Skye in his lap. Gus jumped in after them.

"You're okay, Skye. Calm down, darlin'. There's nothing to be afraid of. Just a couple of idiots with too much to drink."

Skye still shook like she was in a meat locker. He could hear her teeth chatter. "I'm sorry," she said, burying her face against his chest and clinging to him for dear life. "I'm so sorry. I've ruined everything. I'm such a wuss."

"You're not a wuss," Sam said, holding her close. "You just got a little scared. It's okay." He patted her back and rocked her all the way home, murmuring, "It's okay. It's okay. I've got you."

By the time they drove up to the front of the house, Skye's shaking had about stopped. Sam continued to hold her until Gabe got out and unlocked the front door and turned off the alarm. Sam managed to get out of the backseat still holding Skye in his arms.

"Put me down, please," she said. "I can make it by myself."

"I'll carry you."

"Sam, please. I feel stupid enough as it is."

"I'll take care of her," Gabe said. "Belle, would you mind either taking my car or letting Sam drive you home?"

Belle looked sort of funny, but she said, "Sam can drive me."

Flora came hurrying out with Tiger and Pookie. "Is something wrong?"

"A fight broke out at Fancy's," Gabe said, "and Skye got a little frightened. Everything's fine. I'm going to take her upstairs to her room." He whisked Skye inside and left everyone standing on the porch. Except Gus. Gus hurried after them.

Pookie started yapping and jumping up on Sam. He

reached down and scooped her up. "Flora, I hate what happened tonight. Will she be okay?"

Flora patted his arm. "She'll be just fine. Pardon everyone's manners. Did you have fun? Before the fight, I mean?"

Belle laughed. "We had a great time. I didn't know Skye was such a good dancer."

"Oh, yes. She always loved to dance," Flora said. "She was always so lively and gay before— Well, it changed her a great deal. Would you like to come in for a cup of coffee or a drink?"

"No, ma'am," Sam said. "But thanks. I guess we'd better be getting along."

Belle kissed Flora's cheek and told her good night. "Tell Gabe to call me later."

"I will, dear."

Flora went inside, and Belle and Sam climbed into his truck. He set Pookie on Belle's lap. "Sure you don't need a cute dog? She really likes you."

Belle laughed. "Pookie likes everybody."

As he drove his sister back to her place, Sam said, "Is Skye always like that?"

Belle shrugged. "Beats me. I've never seen her in such a state—except maybe at the pool the other day. And that was nothing like this. She was terrified."

"I'm no shrink, but it seems to me that she ought to be over this thing by now. It's been years since she was kidnapped."

"I'm no shrink, either, but I suppose some things are so traumatic that you never get over them," Belle said. "Do you plan to keep on seeing Skye? She's become a dear friend, and I adore her, but she comes with baggage."

"I like her a lot, too, but I don't know. It's something to think about. Are you pissed at Gabe?"

"About what?"

"About the way he focused his total attention on Skye and left you to fend for yourself."

"He knows I can take care of myself. And he feels terribly responsible for Skye."

"Seems a little overly conscientious to me."

Belle didn't say anything, and he figured that she probably agreed with him.

"Are you in love with Gabe?"

"Head over heels."

"Gonna get married?"

"One of these days. I'm in no rush. I'm concentrating on running the *Wimberley Star* right now."

Sam nodded. "You'll do a good job of it. Ever miss the FBI?"

"Lord, no. I was miserable. I hated chasing the bad guys."

Sam laughed. "I love chasing the bad guys."

"I know. That's why you're a top-notch Texas Ranger."

"It's all I ever wanted to be. And being a part of the cold case unit is a dream come true. I sure wish we could solve these coed kidnapping cases. I hope Skye decides to help us."

"Now's not the time to push it," Belle said as they pulled up in front of her townhouse. "Thanks for the ride, little buzzer."

"Want me to come in and check under the beds?"

She laughed. "The only thing you're likely to find is a dust bunny."

Sam waited until she was inside, then headed back toward San Antonio. All the way home he thought about what Belle had said about Skye coming with baggage. He'd thought that he and Julie, his ex-girlfriend, had really had something going, but she'd gone nuts on him about his lifestyle. She'd worried about the danger of his being a Ranger, especially after he was in a shootout with a bunch of escaped convicts one weekend. She'd hated that he rode a motorcycle and went parasailing and everything else exciting that he loved doing. Had said it made her nervous and gave her nightmares.

They'd parted company.

Now, there was Skye. Seemed like she was afraid of everything, so much so that she practically lived in a fortress. Did he want to get mixed up with that sort of woman? And there was Gabe to consider. He was a good friend and very protective of his sister, a little too protective, if you asked him. If things went any further with Skye and didn't work out, his and Gabe's relationship would be strained at best.

Maybe he'd better cool it with Skye.

On the other hand, she was the only witness in a major cold case. He wanted to pursue that.

And then there were her eyes. And the way he felt when he looked at her. And touched her.

And he hadn't even kissed her yet.

Which might be a good thing. He'd back off and keep things platonic. No harm in just being friends. He liked her. And when Belle and Gabe got married, they'd end up being kinfolk.

SKYE FELT LOWER THAN A SOW'S belly. She sat in the window seat of her bedroom, hugging her knees and looking down at moonlight reflecting off the pool. She'd lived with her fears and phobias so long that she'd gotten used to them and had adapted to her bizarre existence.

And that's all that it was: an existence. She didn't have the joy in living that she used to have before that monster kidnapped her. She had ceased to live life at that moment. In a way, she had died as surely as the others had died. He had killed her.

Anger rose up in her. Anger so intense that she shook from the power of it. She wanted to scream and throw things and howl at the moon like a wolf.

She had been a strong, gutsy woman before he'd snatched that from her.

No, he hadn't snatched it from her. She'd allowed the kidnapper to completely change her personality and her life. She hid behind her fears, retreated from the world. Well, she was sick of it. Sick to death of nightmares and anxiety attacks and a need for guards 24/7. Being around Belle, who had a wonderful zest for life, and now Sam, who teased and laughed so easily, had been really good for her.

Sam had been the best thing to come into her life in a long time, and now he was bound to be disgusted with her hysteria and neurotic behavior. A simple bar fight had thrown her into massive panic. This had to stop. Now. She was not a stupid woman. She could conquer this if she put her mind to it.

Skye got up and went to her computer and turned it on. It was time she became proactive instead of being as frightened as a rabbit.

AFTER A SLEEPLESS NIGHT, SKYE was glad that she had a light load that morning. She called her physician and made an appointment with her and had the receptionist reschedule her last patients before noon. She had Napoleon drive her to Dr. Hamilton's office, and the nurse took her right in.

"What seems to be the trouble, Skye?"

"Only the usual. I appreciate your seeing me on such short notice, but the time has come for me to deal with all my phobias. I need help finding the right psychologist or psychiatrist for me. I didn't have good luck in the past, so I want to choose wisely this time, and I don't want another one who is content to overmedicate me. I've read everything I can on my kind of problem, and I'm afraid that I only became more confused. Obviously, post traumatic stress syndrome, which I seem to have, is not in my field."

"Nor mine," Dr. Hamilton said. "But I know an excellent clinical psychologist in Austin who *is* in the field. Shall I call for an appointment? I might convince her to take you tomorrow afternoon. Would that be okay?"

Anxiety tightened her chest, but Skye ignored it. "The sooner, the better."

The doctor excused herself to make the call and returned in a couple of minutes. "I was lucky enough to catch her, and she'll see you in her home office tomorrow afternoon at three. Dr. Barbara Gossett. Here's her address in Austin. Okay?"

Skye clasped her fingers together tightly and took a deep breath. "Okay."

On the way home, Napoleon asked quietly, "Dr. Skye, are you sick?"

"Why do you ask?"

"Not to butt into your business, but you're looking paler than usual, and you went to the doctor. Do you need some medicine? I can go get it for you."

Skye smiled. Napoleon had strung together more words just then than he usually did in an entire day. "I'm okay, but thanks for your concern. I was simply getting some information from Dr. Hamilton. And I'd appreciate it if you kept my visit to her to yourself. I don't want my mother or my brother to worry needlessly."

Napoleon frowned, but he nodded. She knew that she could trust his discretion. She wouldn't have even asked him to drive her to the doctor's office except that her driver's license had probably expired years ago. That was another thing. Having to depend on someone else to drive her was a pain. And letting it lapse was another sign of her submission to her fears. Thinking about it made her doubly angry with herself.

She was still a little shaky after Napoleon dropped her off at home, but, despite vowing never to see another psychologist or psychiatrist, she was determined to give therapy another go. Reclaiming her life would be worth the price. Maybe Belle would drive her to Austin. She didn't want to ask Gabe. She adored her brother, but, bless his heart, he hovered too much.

WHILE THERE WAS A RAIN DELAY on the game on TV, Sam figured that he might as well walk the dog. He clipped on her leash and took Pookie outside for a stroll through the complex of townhouses. A few people were out—mostly kids playing in the commons area.

A little girl about ten or eleven came running over, knelt down in front of the dog and started petting her. "This is Pookie, isn't it? Mrs. Book's dog."

"It is," Sam said. "You know her?"

She nodded. "Mama said she died. My name is Kim. Are you the cop that lives next door to Mrs. Book?"

"Texas Ranger. How'd you know?"

"Mama told me. And I saw that." She pointed to the silver star on his shirt.

Pookie seemed to be great friends with Kim. "I think she likes you."

"She does. Pookie and I played together sometimes when Mrs. Book invited me in for cookies." Kim hugged the little rascal. "And I love her. I wish I had a dog."

Sam's eyebrows when up. Here was a chance to unload Pookie. "Say, how would you like to have Pookie for your very own?"

Kim's face brightened. "I'd like that very much." Just as quickly, her face fell. "But I can't. My little brother is allergic. Cats and dogs make him breathe funny. But can I play with Pookie sometimes?"

"Sure you can." Sam had a thought. "Maybe you can earn some money doing just that. Let's go talk to your mother."

Wonder of wonders, Kim's mother, Donna Baxter, went along with Sam's plan. While he didn't find a new home for Pookie, he found the next best thing. A doggie companion, and at a bargain. Donna agreed to let her daughter stop by after school and play with the dog as well as take her on walks. It was a win-win-win situation. The dog got attention, Kim got to "sort of have a dog," as she put it, as well as earn money, and Sam got to salve his conscience. If he had to work late or go out of town, Kim would see that Pookie got fed and cared for. He left an extra key with Kim and her mother and went home whistling.

The rest of his Saturday dragged by. And Sunday morning wasn't any better. He thought a dozen times about picking up the phone and calling Skye, but each time he told himself to forget it. Not a good idea. Belle was right; Skye came with too much baggage. She wasn't his kind of woman.

But exactly what was his kind of woman?

He'd been attracted to Julie, too. Attracted enough to ask her to marry him, but she was a nervous Nellie sort as well. Scared of her own shadow. Was there something in his character, some protective streak, that drew him to that kind of person?

Maybe, but he'd be better off with someone more like his sister—smart, good-looking, gutsy and fun.

For sure Skye was smart and good-looking, and they'd had fun together before she went nuts on him. Maybe three out of four wasn't bad. And to her favor, he was partial to blondes. Sunday afternoon he thought about driving over to Wimberley. Just for a short visit. Just to check on her.

No. Bad idea. Cool it, Outlaw.

Oh, hell, who was he kidding?

He picked up the phone and called. But Flora told him she and Belle were gone for the afternoon. *Damn.*

Chapter Seven

"Turn left here," Skye told Belle as she directed her up the winding road on Austin's hilly northwest side. Skye had checked the address on her computer and printed out a map and directions.

"Want to tell me now where we're going?" Belle asked.

"We're going, rather I'm going, to see a psychologist. Slow down. Let me check the numbers on the mailboxes."

"And why don't you want your family to know about it?"

"I don't want to cause another stir. It should be just ahead on the right. There. The Spanish-style house. Stop here. Do you mind going to the door and seeing if this is the right place? Do you have your gun?"

Belle looked at her as if she'd grown another head, but Skye couldn't help it. She'd never ventured this far without Gabe or a guard, and she was a basket case. Her anxiety level was off the charts.

"Skye, I don't see why seeing a psychologist would cause a stir. I think they'd be happy that you wanted to get some help. Am I missing something here?"

"I simply wanted to try this out before I got everybody's hopes up. Therapy didn't work for me before. My anxiety seemed to get worse instead of better with one therapist, and the other merely loaded me up on medication until I was a zombie. I'll tell Gabe and Mom if this seems promising. In the meantime, just go along with my story of helping you hang curtains." She squeezed Belle's hand. "Thanks for doing this with me."

"Your hands are freezing. Are you frightened?"

"Terrified, but I'm determined to give this a try. Dr. Hamilton highly recommends her."

"Is her name Gossett?" Belle asked.

"Yes, how did you know?"

"It says Gossett on the mailbox. This must be the place. Come on. I'll walk you to the door."

Skye clenched her teeth and got out of the car, praying that she'd made the right decision. Gus, sensing her anxiety, stayed so close to her that he bumped against her legs as she walked up the path to the split-level stucco.

Belle rang the doorbell, and it was answered almost immediately by a middle-aged woman whose red hair was going to gray. She had the greenest eyes Skye had ever seen, and the corners seemed permanently crinkled from smiling, which she was doing now.

"I'm Barbara Gossett. Which one of you is Skye?" She glanced from one to the other.

"I am."

"I'm just a friend," Belle said. "Skye, I'll wait for you in the car."

Dr. Gossett must have seen the panic that flooded Skye, for she said, "No need for that. Come in. Let's take some time to get acquainted over tea. I even have some cookies. Save me from eating them all."

"I never turn down cookies," Belle said, offering her hand and introducing herself.

The doctor locked the deadbolt behind them, then led them into her office, which had a cozy sitting area with cushy blue chairs across from a large desk and shelves of books. Windows along the back let in sunlight, and French doors led to a sun porch and allowed a glimpse of the pool beyond. Flowers bloomed everywhere in the backyard, and a vase of zinnias sat alongside a tray of iced tea and chocolate-chip cookies on the coffee table.

"What a gorgeous creature you are," Dr. Gossett said to Gus. "May I pet him?"

"Of course, but you might offer Gus your hand first."

The doctor held out the back of her hand to the dog, then stroked his head. "Belle," she said, "would you pour the tea for us?"

Belle poured three of the four glasses full while the psychologist squatted down and scratched Gus's ears and talked baby talk to him. "I used to have a big guy like you, but I've turned into a cat lover these days. How do you feel about cats, Gus? Think they would make a good meal?"

Skye chuckled. "He's very tolerant of cats and all animals. Lucky, since I'm a veterinarian."

"How delightful! I didn't realize that. My late husband was a vet as well. Perhaps you met him at some time. His name was Howard Parvino."

"Of course I knew Dr. Parvino. At least I've heard him and read his work. He was a frequent guest lecturer when I was in school at A&M. I was sorry to hear of his death a few years ago."

"Thank you." She sat down and passed the cookie plate and the three of them chatted for a few minutes. Then she said, "Belle, you might like to take your tea and enjoy the sun porch for a few minutes. There are magazines out there if you'd like to read, and we can see each other through the doors." She turned to Skye. "Okay?"

Skye realized that Dr. Gossett had worked things so that Skye would feel comfortable before Belle left.

Skye nodded. "That's fine." And she did feel comfortable. She liked Dr. Gossett very much, and she had a good feeling about this. They began to talk and, before she knew it, the session was over.

They made an appointment for the following Thursday afternoon, with plans for Skye to see her twice a week for a while.

As she and Belle drove home, Skye felt lighter and more hopeful than she'd felt in a very long time.

GABE WAS NOT SMILING. "YOU'VE been *where?*"

"I've been to see a psychologist," Skye said. "Belle drove me. I like her very much."

"So do I, but I thought you were going to help her hang curtains this afternoon."

"Why should I do that?" Skye asked. "Dr. Gossett has perfectly lovely curtains already up." She bit back her laughter at Gabe's expression. He looked as if he wanted to spout steam from every joint but was fighting hard against it.

"Dammit, Skye! Stop playing games with me. This is serious."

She tiptoed to kiss his cheek. "Don't get in such an uproar, big brother. It's bad for your blood pressure. The reason that I didn't tell you the truth was that I wanted to avoid long, involved discussions before I went to see her. I wanted to check her out first. I did. I like her. And I'm going back next Thursday afternoon. You may drive me if you don't make a fuss. Otherwise, I'll ask Ralph or Napoleon to do it."

He mumbled something.

"I beg your pardon?"

"*I'll* drive you. Why did you pick this particular time to go see another psychologist?"

"Why not? If you'll excuse me, I'm going to run upstairs and change."

"Mom said Sam called while you were gone."

His comment stopped her dead in her tracks. "Oh, really? Sorry I missed him."

"Is Sam the reason for your sudden decision to visit the shrink?"

She felt her face flush. "My decision wasn't sudden. I've been thinking about it for a long time, Gabe. This is no way to live. For any of us."

She hurried upstairs before he could say more.

Or before she could. Gabe had sacrificed so much for her that she didn't want him to think she was ungrateful, but at the same time, she felt a bit rebellious against his overbearing manner. He was only trying to protect her, she reasoned, but still it rankled.

Maybe that was a good sign. She didn't have to be a frightened mouse. She could be a courageous lion.

She chuckled. Or at least a scrappy alley cat.

Belle, who was the gutsiest woman Skye knew, had been a good role model for her. Maybe she'd accept Belle's offer of shooting lessons. Or at least learn karate. Maybe Sam could give her a few pointers in self-defense. Or something. Thinking that he'd called, she smiled. Maybe she should call him back.

SKYE PICKED UP THE PHONE AND put it down a dozen times. She didn't want Sam to think she was pushy.

How dumb. Returning a simple phone call wasn't being pushy. Her meek-mouse attitude had pervaded her life for too long. If she couldn't attack the biggest bugaboos just yet, she could at least start changing the small things.

She sucked in a big breath and dialed his number.

"Outlaw Dogsitters," a deep voice said.

Skye laughed. "Is that a new sideline?"

"Seems to be. Pookie and I have been sitting here watching the ball game, drinking beer and eating potato chips."

"I hope you're teasing about the beer and potato chips."

"Yeah. It's mostly me eating the potato chips. Pookie doesn't care much for them, but she likes beer."

"Are you teaching that poor dog bad habits?"

"I didn't have to teach her anything. She took to the beer

right away, but I explained that she couldn't drink any more until she learned how to open her own. She's over in the corner now, gnawing on a can."

"You're crazy, Sam Outlaw."

"I've been accused of it. You and my sister do anything exciting this afternoon?"

"Does hanging curtains sound exciting?"

"I suppose it depends on who you're hanging them with. I don't have a curtain in the place. Maybe you could come over and help me out sometime."

"It's really not my forte," Skye said.

"Mine, either. Say, have you had dinner?"

"Not yet. Why?"

"I thought I could drive up, and we might go out and grab a pizza or something."

Her stomach seized, then turned. She fought back the feeling. "I don't eat pizza."

"I'm partial to pepperoni and sausage myself, but I think they have vegetarian ones."

"It's not just that. For some reason I can't stand the smell of pizza. Maybe my mother was scared by a delivery man while she was carrying me," she said, trying to be light.

"How do you feel about barbecue?"

"To eat or to smell?"

"Oh, that's right. Meat. Sorry. Is there a Chinese place in Wimberley?"

"Why don't you take pot luck with us? Bring Pookie."

"Hey, Pookie, wanna go see Tiger?"

Pookie barked.

"She says yes. She's already gone to comb her hair."

Skye was still chuckling when she hung up. Nothing might develop between Sam and her, but right now he was very good for her. He made her glow inside. He made her want to be normal.

She hurried to shower and change into something that was pretty, but didn't look as if she fussed. She settled on jeans and a soft blue blouse and was watching from a guest room window when he drove up. She waited to go downstairs until Ralph let him into the foyer.

Sam glanced up as she came down, and the look that he gave her make her heart almost stop. A slow smile spread over his face, and she wanted to fly. She wanted to zip around like Peter Pan and turn cartwheels on the ceiling. Instead, she managed to descend without falling and answered his smile.

"Hi, Sam. I'm glad you could come. Where's Pookie?"

"She split the minute we hit the door. Off to find Tiger, I imagine. I like you in blue. It matches your eyes."

"Thank you."

"Where's Gabe?"

"He's having dinner with Belle tonight. I think Suki and Mother about have our meal ready. Did you bring your appetite?"

"Are you kidding? My appetite is my constant companion. Sure I'm not intruding?"

"Not at all. Sunday nights are pot luck, truly. I think Suki made chili for the meat lovers, and Mom made lentil soup and salad for the rest of us."

"Chili? Lord, I haven't had homemade chili in a coon's age. I love it. Come on, woman, let's get to the table before it's all gone." He hung his white Stetson on the hall rack and offered his arm.

How could she resist this charmer? She took the arm he offered, and they went in for supper.

He ate three bowls full. And after peach cobbler and ice cream, he helped carry dishes into the kitchen.

Suki shooed him out. "I can handle this. You go on about your business."

"Don't mind working for my meal. That was mighty fine chili."

"I'll send some home with you. There's plenty."

"Suki, darlin', you're a woman after my own heart. If I could play the guitar, I'd serenade you."

Flora laughed. "Sam Outlaw, you're a big tease."

"I plead guilty, ma'am. I'm sure your lentil soup was good, too, but I just couldn't pass up that chili."

"I'll send some soup along as well."

"You might as well throw in the last of the peach cobbler," Skye said.

Sam winked at her. "I wouldn't argue with that. Did you make it?"

"Me?" Skye said as they walked into the den. "Not hardly. I'm not much of a cook."

"You don't have to be. You have other fine qualities."

"Name three."

"You're beautiful. You're a brilliant veterinarian. And the way you look at me with that smile of yours makes me break out in a sweat."

"Really?"

"Really. Come on, let's go for a stroll so I can walk off some of that excellent dinner."

"A stroll? You mean outside?"

"Sure."

"But it's dark outside."

"I hope to shout. There's a full moon, and we won't go far."

Skye's heart began to race. That prickly feeling rushed over her. "I—I'd rather not."

Sam drew her close to him, rested his forearms on her shoulders and leaned down to look her square in the eye. "Darlin', trust me, I'd eat ground glass before I'd let anything happen to you. Don't you know that Texas Rangers keep their saddles oiled and their guns greased? I can lick my weight in wildcats. You'll be safe with me."

Still, she hesitated. Even though she believed every word Sam said, old obsessions died hard.

"Come on. Just for five minutes. I might bust if I don't kiss you outside in the moonlight."

Chapter Eight

Taking in a deep breath to fortify her, Skye punched in the numbers to deactivate the alarm. Sam smiled, opened the door and held out his hand. She took it and together they walked out onto the porch. Her knees quivered.

"Think we could leave Gus inside?" Sam asked.

She shook her head. "Where I go, Gus goes."

They walked a few steps away from the house, and Sam looked up at the sky. "Man, look at that moon and those stars. Pretty, isn't it?"

She looked up, losing herself in the stunning sight overhead. "The moon is so full and bright that I want to howl."

"Then do it." He turned her toward him.

"What a ruckus that would cause." She watched as he slowly lowered his mouth to hers, barely brushing her lips gently with his until she put her arms around him and pulled him closer. "I won't break."

"I didn't figure you would, but I want to give Gus some time to get used to the idea."

He kept brushing her lips until she thought she would go out of her mind. It wasn't enough. She pulled his head down and kissed him with all the hunger she felt, molding herself against his big body and losing herself in the feel of his tongue and his mouth and his hands.

Sam Outlaw was awesome, and he set fires in her body—

unbelievable fires—that made her want to do unbelievable things. When he pulled back, she didn't want to break the kiss.

"Whew. Darlin', you are something else." He threw his head back and howled, a long, loud wolf howl.

Laughing, she joined him, throwing back her head and giving a howl like a lobo in the wild.

He howled again. So did she. Gus began barking and growling and grabbed Sam's pant leg.

The front door flew open. Suki, Ralph and her mother raced outside, Suki with her broom and Ralph with a shotgun.

"What in the world is going on?" Flora asked from behind Ralph.

Her shoulders shaking with laughter, Skye hid her face against Sam's shirt.

"We're howling at the moon," Sam said, as if such behavior were perfectly normal. "Want to join us?"

"Sounds a little teched if you ask me," Suki said, taking her broom back inside.

Ralph merely shrugged and followed his wife, but Flora laughed merrily and said, "Sounds like a fine idea to me." She threw her head back and let out a spirited howl, then another. "Feels lovely. Sorry we interrupted. Go on with your howling." She fluttered her fingers and went back inside.

Skye and Sam both burst into laughter.

"I adore your mother," Sam said.

"She's one of a kind."

"So are you. I really like you, Skye Walker."

"I like you, too, Sam."

"Good." He lifted her chin and kissed her again.

Her toes curled, and she melted against him.

"Uh, darlin', could you call off your dog? I'm not going to have a decent pair of jeans left if he keeps this up."

She'd been so engrossed that she hadn't even heard Gus growling and clamping on to the hem of Sam's jeans. "Gus, release! Don't do that again."

SAM HAD TOLD EVERYONE good-night soon after, collected his doggy bag and Pookie and left. Skye almost floated upstairs. She had been becoming very attached to Sam *before* he'd kissed her. Things had escalated considerably.

She couldn't believe that she'd actually gone outside with him at night and hadn't once felt panicky. Maybe because her brain was too befuddled by his kisses. Man, he could kiss. Maybe there was hope for her after all. She'd been tempted to mention having gone to see Dr. Gossett, but she decided to hold off a bit and see how things went before she told him. She was hoping that, with the psychologist's help, not only would she get over her phobias and anxieties, but also she could remember something to help Sam's unit with the kidnappings.

Curling up on the sofa in her sitting room, Skye went through the stack of mail-order catalogs she received almost daily, tossing some and keeping the best. Then she went through the best ones, looking for blue things. Sam liked her in blue.

She found two really cute tops, a skirt and some pants and ordered them online, then turned in, planning to have pleasant dreams of Sam. Gus got in his bed on the floor beside her. Although several nightlights illuminated her rooms, she merely dimmed her bedside lamp and left it burning.

"Good night, boy."

Gus snuffled, the way he always did.

She snuggled in and thought of Sam and the wonderful feeling of his lips on hers. The next thing she knew, lights blazed and Gabe was sitting beside her bed, calling her name and wiping her face with a cool cloth. She was sweating, and her body ached with tension.

"Another nightmare?" she asked her brother.

"Yes," Gabe told her. "A really bad one. Gus was having a fit."

Skye sat up and her hand went to her burning throat. "Was I screaming?"

"Like a banshee." He smiled and handed her a glass of water to quench the fire. "Think you can get back to sleep?"

"What time is it?"

"About one-thirty."

"I have to sleep. I have a full day at the clinic."

"Want me to stay with you for a while?"

"No, I'll be fine. Thanks, Gabe." She squeezed his hand.

After he left, Skye rolled over and stared at the ceiling. She could almost see the face. Almost. But, as it always had, the image quickly faded as she awakened. She was left only with the faint smell of pizza.

Her stomach turned, and she bounded for the bathroom.

"ANY LUCK WITH THE Walker woman?" Heck asked Sam.

Sam shook his head. "Not yet. Her experience spooked her pretty bad," he told his lieutenant. "But she's considering going to a hypnotist. I don't want to push too hard and scare her off completely. I've been reading up on the kind of amnesia she has, and the fact is, lots of people never remember the incident."

"Keep working on it, Sam. Use that famous charm of yours. Never seen a woman yet that you couldn't sweet-talk into anything."

Sam's hackles went up, and he started to shoot back a hot reply, but he held his tongue. He and Heck had been friends a long time, but he was also Sam's boss, and there was no need to advertise that his interest in Skye was any more than as a crime victim.

Just thinking about her, about kissing her—and more—got him so aroused that he was afraid he might be walking around the office straddle-legged if he didn't watch out. He chuckled at the thought. Maybe that was an exaggeration, but not much. Kissing her had sent him soaring, and she hadn't been shy about returning the kiss.

At first he'd thought that Skye was shy. She wasn't shy, only skittish because of all her fears and anxieties. He planned to move very slowly with her for several reasons. For one, he didn't want to get in so deep that he couldn't withdraw easily.

He snorted at that thought. It was obvious where his mind was.

Sam went to his desk and made a few phone calls about another case he was working on. Looked like he was going to have to spend a day or two in Beaumont questioning witnesses.

AFTER THEIR THURSDAY MORNING yoga class, Skye, Belle and Sally Olds, the owner of Head Lines, one of the local hair salons, stopped off for lattes. It had taken Skye a while to be comfortable with only Belle and Gus for protection, but, after all, Belle was an ex-FBI agent, a crack shot and a karate expert, and it was broad daylight. The three of them usually went to the coffee shop after class for some girl talk.

"Sally," Skye asked, "think you could do something a little different with my hair? Something that would be…well, cuter? Do you think I ought to grow it out some?"

"What's with you?" Belle asked. "I always thought you liked easy wash and wear."

"I do, but maybe it's time for a change."

"I think that style is adorable on you," Sally said.

"If you're concerned about impressing Sam," Belle said, "I doubt if he'd notice unless you shaved your head or dyed your hair green. Men are like that."

"I'm not trying to impress Sam. I'm simply considering a change."

"Bangs might do it," Sally said. "Just a little more layering around your face would give you a softer look. Let's go over to Belle's and try it. I don't want to show my face in the shop today or I'll get waylaid by somebody for some emergency."

They all went over to Belle's, Skye sat on a kitchen stool while Sally made magic with the scissors she'd pulled from her enormous shoulder bag.

"Most of my customers would trade their firstborn for hair this natural shade of blond. And you have great body. It's a dream to work with." After a few snips here and there, Sally ruffled Skye's hair and finger combed it. "What do you think?" she asked Belle.

"Fabulous! It really draws attention to her eyes."

"I want to see it," Skye said. She hopped down and went to the bathroom to look. The others followed.

"Well?" Sally said.

Skye turned her head this way and that, then checked the back with a hand mirror. "I really like it. Send me the bill, Sally."

"No bill. I'll trade you for Lucky's next office visit."

"That's a deal." Skye checked her watch. "I've got to run and have a shower and get changed before lunch."

They said goodbye to Sally, and Belle drove her home. Belle walked her to the door as she always did. Skye was about to unlock the front door when Suki opened it.

"Thought I heard you drive up," Suki said. "Gabe just called and said to tell you he got tied up in San Antonio on business. Then something wasn't working just right on the helicopter, and it may take him awhile to get it fixed."

"How long is awhile?"

Suki shrugged. "Don't ask me. I don't know nothing about those things. 'Scuse me, I gotta go check my pie."

"Well, damn!" Skye said. "I wonder if he'll be able to take me to my appointment with Dr. Gossett."

"What time is your appointment?" Belle asked.

"Two-thirty. I'll see if Ralph can drive me."

"If you have problems," Belle said, "let me know. I can drive you to Austin."

"Thanks, but I know you have an important meeting this afternoon."

"Meetings can be rescheduled. Call me if you need me. Promise?"

Skye nodded. "Thanks."

Belle left and all the time that Skye was resetting the alarm, the thought was running through her head that Gabe might be sabotaging her appointment with the psychologist. Why was he so resistant to her starting therapy again?

Less than an hour later, Gabe called. Sure enough, he wouldn't be back in time to drive her to Austin, and the chopper was down for a half day repair job.

Ralph had driven to Marble Falls to visit a cousin who was in the hospital, so he wasn't available, and her mother was out for the day. Suki was a possibility, but she was a terrible driver, and Skye didn't feel very safe with only her along. She didn't want to make Belle miss her meeting, and it was Napoleon's day off.

Damn.

She tried calling Napoleon, but she couldn't reach him. She considered asking the gate guard or the man on patrol to drive her, but Gabe would skin the poor men alive if one of them left their posts. As a last resort she called Belle, but the person who answered at the newspaper office said that she'd already left for a meeting. Skye didn't try to reach Belle on her cell phone, she didn't want to upset her plans.

Disappointment almost overwhelmed her. There was no choice but to call Dr. Gossett and cancel.

Why, when she had felt so good about this, had her plans been frustrated? She glanced upward. "Help me here. What can I do?"

The heavens didn't part, nor did a guardian angel appear.

She sighed and reached for the phone to cancel her appointment when it rang.

"Hello."

"How's my favorite vet?" Sam asked.

"Frustrated."

"Want to tell me about it? I'm just leaving San Marcos PD, and I can be there in twenty minutes. Fifteen if I hurry."

"Do you have wings?"

He laughed. "Not the last time I looked, but I've got a heavy foot. What's up?"

"I have an important appointment in Austin, and I don't have a ride. Are you available as a chauffeur?"

"You betcha. I'm on my way."

Chapter Nine

"I appreciate this Sam," Skye said as they headed out of Wimberley. "I really didn't want to miss this appointment."

"No problem. Glad I was within range. Mind telling me where we're going?"

Looking nervous, she hesitated.

Being skittish again, Sam thought. "I don't mean to pry into your business, but if I'm going to drive you somewhere, it would help to know where I'm going."

"I understand. We're going to a house in the northwest part of Austin. Just head up Mo-Pac to twenty-two-twenty-two. I'll show you the way from there."

Sam nodded and didn't push for more information. One thing he'd already learned about Skye: she'd tell him more when she was good and ready. "Say, I like your hair. Is that a new do?"

She lit up with a big smile. "Yes. I'm surprised you noticed."

"I noticed. It's pretty. Shows off your eyes."

"Thanks. Uh, I'm going to an appointment with Dr. Gossett. She's a psychologist."

Careful here. "That's good. She practice out of her house?"

"Not usually. She's arranged her schedule so that she can take a long lunch break and see me at her home on Thursdays.

I'm going to see her on Sunday afternoons, too. I really like Dr. Gossett. I think that maybe she can help me."

Sam nodded. "That's good." He wanted to shout "hallelu-jah!" but he kept his mouth shut. Heck would be glad to hear about the progress and forgive him for bailing this afternoon.

SKYE WAS GRATEFUL that Sam didn't push her about delving into her memories. That was one of the things she and Dr. Gossett were going to discuss, along with the nightmares.

When they arrived, she introduced Sam as Belle's brother and a friend. Dr. Gossett was as warm and friendly to Sam as she had been to his sister on Sunday. After chatting for a few minutes, the psychologist sent Sam onto the sun porch to read, and their session began.

Skye found it very easy to pour out her frustration with her fears and phobias and relate her nightmares.

"It sounds as if you're really ready to go to work," the doctor said.

"I am."

They talked a while longer, and Dr. Gossett said, "I think hypnosis would be an excellent tool to use with you. We'll use some other techniques as well, but from what I understand of your history, I believe that hypnosis will be very helpful. Have you ever been hypnotized before?"

"Yes. Another psychologist tried it with me, but I wasn't very responsive. It didn't work."

Dr. Gossett chuckled. "That person obviously didn't have my special techniques. We'll go slowly and get you used to the state. I think you're going to be an excellent subject."

She had Skye kick back in the high leg recliner she sat in, then put a small neck roll behind her head and covered her legs with a light throw. She turned on a sound machine with muted ocean effects of waves breaking on the shore and started talking very softly in a measured tone, her voice as soothing as summer breeze.

Skye began drifting and relaxing until she felt totally boneless, as if she were floating on a cloud. She felt wonderful as she went deeper and deeper into very relaxed feelings, listing to the sound of the doctor's voice and following directions because she chose to. Deeper and…

"ONE, TWO, THREE. Open your eyes. Wide awake. Feeling great."

Skye blinked open her eyes. She stretched. "I feel great. I can't remember when I've been so relaxed. Was I hypnotized?"

"Absolutely," Dr. Gossett said. "For over half an hour."

Skye startled. "Half an hour? I can't believe it. It felt more like five minutes."

"Do you remember the cue word I gave you?"

"Yes. Buttermilk." Skye chuckled. "Will saying it actually help?"

"Of course. When you feel an anxiety attack coming, simply close your eyes for a moment and say the word, and you'll slip into the very relaxed state you're feeling now. You can't be relaxed and anxious at the same time. I promise it will work."

"That's terrific. I'll try it."

"Good." Dr. Gossett stood. "You did very well. Given a little time, I think we can lick your problems."

Skye stood as well. "So do I."

"Just don't sign any contracts today or buy any snake oil. You might find yourself still a bit suggestible for a few hours. And I predict that you're going to sleep well tonight."

Spontaneously, Skye hugged Dr. Gossett. "Thank you."

"My pleasure."

A few minutes later, Sam and Skye were headed back home.

"Things go well?" Sam asked.

"Very well. I feel fantastic."

"Want to stop by the pie place for a piece of pie and a cup

of coffee? I've got a hankering for chocolate. Or maybe pecan."

Her old panic hit.

Oh, no. Despair flooded her. Then she closed her eyes, took a deep breath and said, "Buttermilk."

Her muscles relaxed and the panic faded.

"I'm not sure they have buttermilk, but we can check."

Skye chuckled. "Sounds good to me."

As it turned out, the place didn't have buttermilk—Sam asked—so she settled for water and a sinful piece of lemon meringue pie. Sam ate two pieces of chocolate and bought a whole pie to take home with him, plus a lemon, a chocolate and a pecan for Skye's family.

"This is very sweet of you," Skye said as they carried the boxes to the car.

"Not sweet, just good politics. It's payback for the chili and stuff. And, you never know, I might get invited to stay for supper."

FLORA BEAMED AS SAM handed her the pies. "What a dear, thoughtful boy you are! You must stay for dinner. Or do you have to get back to Rangering?"

"No, ma'am. I can stay."

"Wonderful! Let's take these to the kitchen. I'm baking yeast rolls."

"Yes, ma'am. I could smell them the minute I walked in the door. I'm a fool for yeast rolls."

"I don't bake often, but I felt a sudden yen this afternoon. Maybe it was because the ones we had at our luncheon left something to be desired."

"I'm going to run upstairs for a moment," Skye said.

"You go right ahead, darlin'," Sam said. "I'll keep your mama company."

Flora tittered. "Oh, Sam, you're such a card. You must let me paint you."

"Yes, ma'am. What color did you have in mind?"

Her lilting laughter followed her as she led the way to the kitchen.

"You must have come from Uranus. You're such a composite of opposites. Tough as they come but as sweet as one of these lovely pies. I think you're very good for my Skye. Just don't hurt her badly, Sam, or I might have to break your legs."

Chuckling, he said, "I think you just might."

"Don't ever doubt it for a minute. But I don't think I have to worry about it. What happened to Gabe?"

"I think his chopper got grounded in San Antonio."

"And he sent you?"

Sam shook his head. "I just happened to call Skye from San Marcos, and she told me she needed a ride. Lucky accident."

"Don't fool yourself, my dear boy," Flora said as she pulled a pan of rolls from the oven. "Somebody's guardian angel was behind this. Skye's, I suspect. I often think that her father watches out for her."

Sam snatched a roll from the pan. "Really?"

"You'll burn your fingers doing that."

He tossed the roll from hand to hand. "Not likely. I've got this down to a fine art."

"What?" Skye asked as she came in.

"Hot roll filching."

Skye shoved the butter dish toward him, handed him a knife and climbed on a stool at the kitchen island.

He slathered butter on the roll and ate it in two chomps. "Oh, Flora darlin', these are pure heaven. Will you marry me?"

"Not in this lifetime, but I'll let you have another roll."

The three of them sat at the island and polished off the entire pan of rolls with Flora making sketches of Sam as he ate.

Gabe came in just as Flora was putting another pan of rolls in the oven along with a couple of casseroles from the refrigerator. He kissed Flora and Skye and shook hands with Sam.

"What are you doing here, Sam? Not that you're not welcome, you understand."

"Playing angel. You get your helicopter fixed?"

"No, I had to leave it and rent a car. Skye, I'm sorry that I missed our lunch and appointment."

"No problem," Skye said. "Sam took me, and everything worked out fine. Isn't he a sweetheart?"

"I'm not sure I'd categorize him as that," Gabe said, "but thanks, buddy. I was going to give you a call and see how you felt about a fishing trip this weekend up at your lakehouse."

"Sounds good to me. When do you want to leave?"

"How about early Saturday morning? We can spend the night and fish awhile on Sunday morning. The chopper should be ready tomorrow, and we can fly up."

"I'll get my gear ready," Sam said. "How about you ladies? Want to go fishing? I know Belle loves to fish."

Gabe looked a little pained, but he kept his mouth shut, hoping, Sam figured, that they would decline.

Skye beamed. "I'd love to go. I haven't been fishing in ages."

"You've never been fishing," Gabe said. "And don't you have appointments on Saturday morning? Besides, Belle can't go. She has a publisher's seminar in Dallas this weekend."

Skye's face fell a mile, and Sam wanted to kick his friend.

"You ladies can still go," Sam said. "How about you, Flora? Want to go drown a few worms?"

"Sounds ghastly to me," Flora said. "Besides, Saturday is a busy day at the gallery, and I can't leave this weekend."

"Maybe another time," Skye said, offering a sad little smile that nearly melted Sam's heart. "I do have patients to see."

"You up to trying Fancy's again tomorrow night?" Sam

asked her. "I could come up and spend the night so Gabe and I can get an early start on our trip."

He watched a play of emotions across her face, then she said, "Sure. That would be fun. I'll try not to freak out on you this time."

Chapter Ten

Nothing like double-dating with your mother and your brother, Skye thought as she applied lip gloss. She shrugged. Oh, well.

Belle had already left for her seminar in Dallas, and Gabe wouldn't hear of her going without him. "I'll be your date," Flora had said.

Gabe had looked horrified. "Mom, we're going boot scootin' at Fancy's."

"What? You think I can't scoot my boots? I can run you into the ground, dear boy. Unless you're embarrassed to be seen dancing with your mother."

Skye stifled a giggle as Gabe quickly said, "Of course not."

"Good. That's settled."

She must have said "buttermilk" a thousand times since her session with Dr. Gossett the day before, but it always seemed to quell her moments of anxiety if she followed directions. It was a great technique, but she knew it was only a temporary bandage for the real work to be done.

It would do for now.

She took a deep breath, said "buttermilk" and went downstairs.

SAM HAD NEVER HAD so much fun in his life—even with a dog chaperone. Not only was he sporting the best-looking woman in the room, her mother could dance rings around people half her age, and she was a pistol. No wonder Skye was such a winner. Since he hadn't slept much the night before, by ten o'clock he was flagging, but when the band struck up a slow waltz, he pulled Skye to her feet.

"Ready for another go?"

She smiled up at him and he nearly let out a rebel yell. Man, when she turned on that smile, his heart went marching to Georgia, and he could have danced all night with her in his arms.

After they took a couple of whirls around the floor, he said, "Are you having a good time?"

"Fabulous. I don't think even a fight breaking out would bother me tonight."

"Good." He pulled her closer, tucked her head under his chin and waltzed as if he held a feather in his arms. Except that she didn't feel like a feather against his body. He felt every soft curve that pressed him as they danced. He could have held her forever except that the music stopped and the band took a break.

When they returned to the table, Gabe said, "Y'all about ready to go? Five o'clock is going to come early in the morning."

Sam watched Skye's face fall, and he nearly told Gabe what he could do with his fishing trip. "It's up to the ladies. I'm just getting my second wind."

"It's getting late," Skye said, "and we all have to get up early. We'd better go."

"I think that's wise," Flora said, but she looked wistfully at the dance floor.

Even Gus moved slowly as they all left and went to the car.

"How about we do this again next Friday night?" Sam said.

Skye brightened. "I'd love it."

When they returned to the house, Gabe excused himself to

call Belle, and Flora quickly said good-night and went upstairs, leaving Sam and Skye alone in the foyer.

"I really had fun tonight," she told him. "I wasn't nearly as nervous as I thought I'd be."

"No fights."

Skye smiled. "I think we left before things started getting too frisky. I wasn't worried. I've known most of the people there all my life."

"Wanna go outside and look at the stars?" Sam asked.

"Is that a subtle way of asking to kiss me?"

"Funny, I've never been accused of being subtle. Or of asking for kisses." He lowered his mouth to hers. Gus growled softly. Sam ignored him.

Their lips barely touched when a bloodcurdling scream came from upstairs.

They jerked apart, and Sam shot up the stairs, taking the steps two at a time. "Stay there," he shouted to Skye over his shoulder.

She didn't listen, and he was surprised that she came running behind him, Gus beside her and barking. "It's just Mother. She probably saw a scorpion. Or thought she did. She's phobic about them."

Sam had his boot gun drawn when he flung open the door and scanned the room. "What's wrong?"

Flora stood on a chair, clutching her chest and looking ashen. "A scorpion in my bathroom. I'm terrified of them, and they seem to know it and single me out. Do something, Sam. But don't shoot it. You'll ruin the tub."

"Yes, ma'am." Once in Flora's bathroom, he spotted a small scorpion in the bottom of her tub, stepped on it, then picked it up with a tissue and flushed it down the toilet. He stuck his gun back in his boot.

When he exited the bathroom, he heard Flora saying, "See, I told you that Manuel hadn't been spraying properly. I don't know why I'm the only one who sees them around here."

Skye looked skeptical, but Sam said, "They must have found a way into your bathroom. I used to have a problem with them at the lake house, but a friend told me about a product to use around the outside of the house, and it did the trick. I'll write the name of it down and you can tell Ralph or Manuel."

"Oh, would you, dear boy?" Flora climbed down and patted Sam's cheek. "To finally be rid of those awful creatures would be a blessing."

Gabe stuck his head in. "Another scorpion sighting?"

"I have it under control," Sam said.

"I've got to go and call Belle back."

"Tell her we said, 'hey,'" Sam said.

Flora smiled sweetly. "Thank you, again, Sam, and good night, dears."

Sam walked Skye to her door, and Gabe hurried downstairs.

"Let's see," Sam said, "where were we when the screaming started?"

Skye lifted her face and brushed her lips against his. "About here, as I recall."

Flora's door opened, and she stuck her head out. "Sam you forgot to write the name— Oops. Sorry." The door quickly closed.

Sam chuckled. "Looks like we're snake-bit tonight." He dropped a quick kiss on her mouth. "I'll see you when we get back."

SAM'S BASS BOAT LAY ANCHORED in a cove at Lake Travis. He'd just made a cast into the sweet spot that had already yielded four nice fish.

"Sam," Gabe said. "I need to get something straight with you."

"Okay. Shoot."

"It's about Skye. I'm worried."

"About what?" Sam asked as he reeled in his lure. "Something wrong with her?"

"There's a lot wrong with her, but what I'm worried about is you and her."

"Haven't we had this conversation before?"

"Yeah, but I don't think you fully gasped the seriousness of the situation," Gabe said.

"What situation?"

"Dammit, Sam! Skye has serious emotional problems, and she's a high-maintenance woman. Do you have any idea of the cost involved just in salaries for guards?"

"You make your sister sound like a spoiled nut case. Sure she has some problems after what she's been through, but she's going to that psychologist now, and she thinks it's helping her. And if you ask me, I think she'll feel a lot better when she can face the memories of what happened to her."

"She'll feel better or you'll feel better? You'd like to crack that case, wouldn't you?"

Sam threw down his rod and jumped to his feet, rocking the boat. "What the hell are you accusing me of, Gabe?"

"I'm not— Hey! Watch your line! You've got a bite." Gabe made a lunge for the rod and reel just as it flew out of the boat. His feet tangled in something, and, arms flailing, Gabe pitched into the water with a loud splash.

Sam roared with laughter as Gabe went under. He was never going to let him forget this. It was almost worth losing his favorite reel to see the look on his buddy's face when he went airborne.

Ready with a dig, he waited for Gabe to surface.

He didn't come up.

"Gabe! Where the hell did you go?" Figuring that Gabe was playing a joke, he looked on the other side of the boat, but he didn't see anything. He shouted again.

Nothing.

Oh, hell.

Sam quickly shucked his boots and pants and dove in.

He saw something moving in the dark water and went

deeper. Gabe. He was hung up on a snag of some kind and struggling.

Sam wrenched him loose, and they shot for the surface.

"About damned time," Gabe said, gasping for air. "What got me?"

"An octopus, I think. Can you make it to the boat?"

"Of course I can make it to the boat. It's only ten feet away."

Sam wasn't so sure. Gabe looked a little green around the gills to him, but they finally made it to where Gabe could hang on to the side and catch his breath. Sam helped his friend into the boat and hoisted himself in as well.

Gabe lay in the bottom, panting, and Sam sat on an ice chest, hunched over and dripping.

"Shame you couldn't save my rod and reel," Sam said.

"To hell with your rod and reel! I'll buy you a new one. A dozen new ones. What was I hung up on?"

"Looked to me like a spinnerbait tied to a lawn chair."

"A *lawn chair?*"

"Yep."

"How in the hell did a lawn chair end up in the lake? And with a spinnerbait attached to it?"

"Beats me. Bet it would make an interesting story. Roll over on your side. I think the lure's still attached to your belt loop in the back."

Sam stripped off his wet T-shirt and got a pair of clippers from his tackle box. He cut the barbs and pulled the lure free from where it had embedded itself in the back of Gabe's pants. He held it up.

"Looks like a Texas Two Stepper to me," Sam said. "I think I'm going to frame it. Say, maybe we can get our picture taken at the marina. I'll bet I've beaten the lake record. What do you weigh?"

Gabe started laughing, and Sam joined in. When the laughs finally died down, Gabe said, "Sam, you saved my life. Thanks."

"Glad to oblige. Belle would have never forgiven me if I'd let you drown. What say let's go back to the house and change clothes? I've lost one of my damned socks. Did you lose your billfold?"

Gabe slapped the side of his cargo pants. "No, it's zipped up in here, and my keys are on the dresser, so I'm good except for my shoes. They're gone. I notice that you took time to undress."

"Made for better maneuvering. And I didn't want to ruin my best fishing pants." Sam pulled on his ragged jeans and started the engine. "I'm hungry. How about we heat up some of that chili Suki sent along?"

SAM AND GABE HAD SPENT THE rest of the day fishing and drinking too much beer. By the time Sam crawled into bed that night, he figured that he'd be out before his head hit the pillow, but for some reason he was wide awake.

Well, not for *some* reason. For one specific reason. Thinking about Skye kept him awake—as it did lots of nights lately. Gabe hadn't brought up the subject of Skye again, but something that his friend had said ate at him. Now, Sam wasn't anywhere near thinking about proposing to her, but it never hurt to have your eyes wide open when you went into a relationship. He'd learned that lesson with Julie. No way could he have lived with their differences, and the issues with Skye made the problems with Julie look minor in comparison.

Just thinking about the security force Gabe provided for Skye blew Sam's mind. Three shifts of two or three guards a shift must cost a chunk of change—way more than a Ranger's pay could cover. Of course he always had the oil lease money that he'd invested, but that would be a drop in the bucket when you had to shell out a bundle every two weeks for payroll. Just thinking about it made his belly knot up.

Even though she seemed very down to earth and undemanding, Gabe was right about Skye. She was a high-maintenance woman. And that wasn't what he was looking for.

Cool it, Sam, just cool it.

Chapter Eleven

Skye had spent plenty of Saturday nights alone, but that one was the worst, and she was still miffed at her brother for discouraging her from going on their fishing trip. She guessed they needed a guy outing, but she'd actually been excited about the prospect.

Gabe had been right, she supposed, about her freaking out somewhere during the weekend. Gabe was usually right, much as it irritated her to admit it. Though she thought her therapist might question that supposition. This was something she wanted to talk with Barbara on Sunday afternoon. Saturday night Skye contented herself with painting her fingernails with pale pink polish, watching TV and reading a veterinarian journal.

On Sunday, she'd planned to go to early church, hoping to be home in time to see Sam when they got back from their trip, but she got an emergency call just as they were about to leave. Alice Eason's toy poodle was in terrible distress, and Alice, an elderly widow, was sure that Taffy was dying.

Skye, along with Suki and Ralph, rushed to the clinic to meet Alice. One look at the poodle, followed by a quick examination, was enough to alert Skye to the problem. Taffy was pregnant and trying to deliver her pups.

"But she can't be pregnant!" Alice exclaimed.

"She is," Skye told her, "and I need to do a C-section."

Shortly afterward, Skye delivered three puppies that were much too large for the toy to birth normally; two were black, and one was the same apricot color as Taffy.

When Skye finished up and left Taffy recovering, she showed the puppies to Alice. "What *are* those?" exclaimed Alice.

"They're puppies."

"Well, I *know* that they're puppies. I mean what kind of breed? I can't imagine how Taffy got exposed. She's always in the house with me, and I only let her out briefly to do her business in the backyard. And I have a very high fence."

"It's too early to tell what kind of dog the sire might be, but I can say he's a champion fence jumper."

Alice looked horrified. "But—but that would mean that he's a very *big* dog."

"Stands to reason."

"But how could he…could she…could they…"

Skye shrugged. "Looks like they managed. Any black dogs nearby?"

"Only that black mongrel that belongs to Elfriede Hutto. And I'm going to give her a piece of my mind, believe you me."

"Are you going to be able to take care of the puppies?" Skye asked.

Alice look doubly horrified. "Heavens, no! What would I do with puppies? You'll just have to—" She fluttered her fingers. "When can I take Taffy home?"

"Let's see how she's doing tomorrow."

"Very well, if you insist. You can send your bill to Elfriede."

Skye watched Alice march to the front door, where Ralph waited to let her out, and sighed.

"Looks like we got ourselves three new mouths to hand feed," Suki said. "And a bill to eat. That Alice Eason hasn't got the sense that God gave a billy goat. If she'd had her dog fixed like you told her to, she wouldn't have gotten in this situation to begin with. Want me to stir up some formula?"

"If you don't mind. I can't think of any dogs that might wet nurse. Let me call Doc Harvey and see if he knows of one."

He didn't. Looked like bottle feeding unless a wet nurse appeared from out of nowhere. Skye checked on Taffy, then bundled up the little trio and took them back to the house.

On the way, Gabe's helicopter buzzed them, and they all waved. "Do you need to pick them up, Ralph?" Skye asked.

"No, they left Sam's truck down by the pad."

"I hope they got a nice mess of fish," Suki said. "I told those boys that I was in the mood for some fried catfish. I'll go heat the grease just in case. The potato salad and cole slaw are already made, and I left a pot of beans simmering. They ought to be ready."

"And if they didn't catch any fish?" Skye asked.

"Then I guess we'll have one of them vegetarian meals with you. Where you gonna put those pups?"

"In my bathroom. They'll be safe there, and the heat lamp will keep them warm."

"You don't mean to do all the night feeding yourself, do you? You won't be fit for anything if you have to get up every three or four hours."

"Maybe I won't have to. I'm still hoping for a wet nurse to show up. I've sent out a call."

Suki rolled her eyes, and Skye chuckled.

Once upstairs in her bathroom, she prepared a box for the puppies.

"How do you feel about being a foster parent, Gus?" Skye asked as she transferred the squirming little things to the soft nest of towels.

Gus sniffed at them, then looked up at her as if to say, "What are these things?"

Laughing, she ruffled his coat. "Come on, fella, let's go get some food for them."

Just as she was about to open the door, there was a knock on it. Startled, her heart lurched.

"You in there?" Sam asked from the other side. "I've got bottles of stuff."

Opening the door, she found Sam in a ball cap and ragged jeans carrying three small bottles of formula.

"Hi, how did the fishing go?"

"Great. Suki's about ready to fry the first batch. I hear you have some new babies."

"I do. Or rather Taffy does. Come on in and you can help me feed them. Have you ever bottle-fed a puppy or a kitten?"

"Not that I recall, but I bottle-fed a calf once."

"Same principal. Smaller critters."

The two of them sat cross-legged on the floor, and Sam, after a few instructions and false starts, fed one of the black pups while Skye fed the other two.

"What kind of dogs are these?" Sam asked. "They look like little rats."

Skye chuckled. "They'll be cute when they get a little bigger. They're half apricot toy poodle and half…something else."

"What happened to the mother?"

"She had to have a C-section." Skye told him the story of Alice Eaton and Taffy.

"So the woman doesn't want the pups? What's going to happen to them?"

"I'll find homes for them when they're old enough to wean."

"And you're going to have to hand feed them until then?" Sam asked.

"Hopefully, a wet nurse will show up to take care of the feeding."

"A wet nurse? From where?"

Skye shrugged. "I'm not sure."

When the little tummies were full, they left the pups snuggled together and sleeping.

"Suki insisted that I stay and eat," Sam said. "And she didn't have to twist my arm much. You going to the therapist this afternoon?"

"Yes, I'd planned to."

"Want me to drive you?"

"Sure, if you don't mind."

"I don't mind. Let me get cleaned up, and I'll meet you downstairs."

SAM HADN'T INTENDED TO STAY. In fact, he'd decided to grab his stuff and Pookie and head back to San Antonio, put a little distance between Skye and him. But one thing had led to another, and, before he knew it, they were driving away from the therapist's house in Austin with Gus sitting in the backseat of his truck.

Maybe it was feeding those little mutts that had short-circuited his brain and made his heart turn to mush. Skye had been so damned cute sitting on the floor feeding the puppies. Her face had glowed as she'd held the bottles to the little mouths, and she'd smiled at him in that heart-stopping way she had, and well…all his good intentions had gone out the window. After lunch, he'd driven Gus and her to Austin, and she'd insisted on hearing all about their fishing trip. He'd even told her about Gabe going overboard, and Skye had laughed until tears came to her eyes. Of course, the real story wasn't nearly as funny as he'd told it, but he gussied it up some for her. The more she'd laughed, the more he'd embellished the truth. He liked to hear her laugh.

Damn, he told himself when he felt a goofy smile on his face just looking at her, he needed to get hold of himself and back off. He was going to have to start repeating "high-maintenance woman" to himself like a mantra until it stuck.

He'd start first thing tomorrow. He was enjoying himself too much today.

"Want to stop for some pie?" he asked her.

"I'd love to, but I'd better get back to the puppies. I had thought that…"

"What?"

"Never mind," she said, but Sam thought that she seemed preoccupied as they scanned the surroundings.

Halfway to Dripping Springs, his curiosity got the better of him and he said, "Did your session go okay?"

"It went great. Barbara says that I'm a really good hypnosis subject."

"Oh?" Sam itched to find out all the details, but he didn't push. He'd already learned that Skye had a stubborn streak.

She chuckled.

"What?"

"You're so transparent. You're dying to know what went on, aren't you?"

He started to fib a little, then thought better of it and only smiled.

"We worked on my phobias some more. She said that maybe in the next week or two, she'll try some regression, but she doesn't want to rush things. She thinks— Sam! Stop. Pull over here."

Sam slammed on his brakes and pulled over to the shoulder. "What's wrong?"

"See that dog?"

He peered all around, then spotted a scruffy-looking dog sitting in the shade of a bush beside the road. "What about him?"

"Her."

"How can you tell this far away?"

"I just can. Pull down a little."

He pulled forward until they were even with the dog, a flea-bitten-looking thing that wouldn't take any prizes at Westminster. Skye opened her door, and the dog started toward them.

"What are you doing?"

"I'm taking her home with us."

"We can't just pick her up. She probably belongs to somebody around here."

"She doesn't."

Skye whistled in a funny sort of way and pulled her seat forward. And the damnedest thing, that mangy-looking mutt jumped into the truck and sat down on the backseat next to Gus, looking proud as a blue ribbon winner. Skye leaned over and petted the dog and cooed to her, and Sam could swear that the dog smiled. He could also see that she was heavy with milk.

"Let's go," Skye said.

"Honey, we can't just take this dog. She's got puppies somewhere."

"She doesn't. They're gone."

"How do you know? Whose dog is this?"

Skye sighed. "Mine now, but I'll put an ad in the paper if it will make you feel better. Just drive."

Sam shook his head. Be a hell of a thing if he got arrested for dognapping, but he didn't argue.

When they got back to Wimberley, Skye asked him to stop by the clinic. She fed and watered the new dog, checked on Taffy, then gave the mutt a good bath and dried her. It didn't help her looks much.

"She doesn't have any tags," Sam said.

"No, but I think I'll call her Nana." The dog must have liked the idea because she yipped and licked Skye's chin. Skye laughed and stroked Nana's head. "Let's get you home. I know three little guys who're going to be glad to see you."

"You snatched her for a wet nurse?"

"Sam, I didn't *snatch* her. She was abandoned, and she chose to come with me. She's perfect. You'll see."

Skye was right.

Nana climbed into the box in Skye's bathroom, nosed the pups around a bit, and soon they were nursing as if she was their mother.

Sam stood with his hands on his hips, watching. "Well, I'll be."

Skye tiptoed and gave him a quick kiss. "Yes, you will."

"There's something special between you and animals, isn't there?"

"Yes. Want some ice cream?" She turned and walked away before he could answer.

He wasn't willing to let it go at that and stopped her in the sitting room. "Skye, how did you know about that dog? You'd been watching for her, hadn't you?"

She shrugged. "I'm no Dr. Dolittle if that's what you're getting at. I'd hoped a wet nurse would show up. She did. I'm grateful."

"And while we're on the subject," Sam said, "something else has been bothering me. How far were you found from where you were abducted?"

"That doesn't seem to be on the subject at all, but I believe it was about five or six miles. Gabe can tell you exactly."

"And your dog found you that far away?"

"Yes. Kaiser was a good tracker."

"He must have been a superdog. Skye, I've never even heard of a bloodhound, much less a German shepherd, that could track a *car* for five miles."

She shrugged again. "Lucky for me that Kaiser was a superdog. We had a special affinity. Do you want yours with whipped cream or without?"

"What are you talking about?"

"I'm talking about ice cream. Are you a chocolate or vanilla man?"

"I'm not picky, but I'll have to pass today. I need to get my stuff and get home. Tomorrow I'm leaving bright and early for El Paso."

"For how long?" she asked.

"I'm not sure. A few days. Depends on how things pan out on a case there. And I'm hoping that I'll have a chance to go caving in the area with some friends."

"Caving?"

"You know, exploring caves. Spelunking."

Her eyes got big, and if he wasn't mistaken, a slight sneer lifted her upper lip. "You mean *underground?* Why on earth would you do that?"

"Because I love it. Caving is a hobby of mine. Do you have a problem with it?"

She flinched, and he wanted to kick himself for being so short and defensive, but that had been another bone of contention between Julie and him. She'd hated the idea of his exploring, and he loved it.

Skye smiled brightly. "Not at all."

"Gabe tells me there are a couple of small caves on the property here. Maybe we can check them out sometime."

Her smile died, and she didn't answer for a moment. "I tend to be a little claustrophobic, but you're certainly welcome to explore to your heart's content. What are you going to do with Pookie while you're gone?"

"I've got a neighborhood kid who comes in to feed her and play for a while."

"Why don't you leave her here with us? Tiger loves the company, and she's no trouble."

Sam debated the options, then decided Pookie would be better off with Skye and her family so he agreed.

"I hope you'll be back by Friday," Skye said.

He frowned. "Friday?"

Skye looked a little disturbed, and he wanted to kick himself again. Why was he always putting his foot in it with her?

"We're supposed to go dancing again," she said. "Don't tell me you've forgotten."

"Forgotten? Not a chance. But the truth is, I may get hung up in El Paso. I'll give you a call later in the week." He dropped a kiss on her nose, and her arms went around him as she lifted her mouth to him.

If he was smart, Sam would grab his dog and his duffle and make tracks. But then, nobody had ever accused him of being Einstein. And her mouth looked too sweet to resist.

And it was sweet. Warm and soft and sweet. He couldn't get enough. Not even Gus's low growls could make him back off. He wanted more, lots more, and his hands slid over her bottom to lift her up and pull her closer to him.

She moaned, and he nearly went nuts.

He caught her hand as it slid under his shirt and managed to tear his lips from hers. "I think I'd better go take a shower."

"Need some company? I'll wash your back."

"Oh, darlin', don't tempt me." He took each of her hands in his, kissed the backs and hot-footed it to his room before he did something totally nuts.

Chapter Twelve

As she lay in bed that night, Skye's mind was buzzing like a hornet's nest. She was sure that Sam thought that she was crazy. Certifiable. It was bad enough that she had a bushel of phobias and was surrounded by a phalanx of bodyguards. Now, after this thing with Nana, the wet nurse, well, that must have put the stamp on it for sure. Things that seemed so natural to her seemed odd to other folks—sort of in the woo-woo realm.

While she adored her mother, lots of people thought Flora was a bit of a kook, and Skye didn't want to be put in the same category. She sighed, turned over and punched her pillow. But people thought she was a kook anyhow, and they didn't even know about the other weird stuff.

But she was who she was, and some things simply came with the territory. She could work on the fears and phobias, but she couldn't do much about the other. Her therapist seemed to think that once she confronted the basic trauma of her abduction, including recalling the person who did it, she would be well on her way to recovery. She'd heard that before, and it made sense. That afternoon they had made a little headway.

The smell of pizza had been almost overpowering. Literally. It had disturbed her so badly that Barbara had brought her out of hypnosis. The scent of it lingered still, and her stomach turned merely remembering. What was it about the combination of sauce and crust and cheese and olives and onions that upset her so?

She got up to go check on Nana and the puppies just to get her mind off it.

The dogs were fine, of course.

Sinking into a rocking chair in the corner of her bedroom, she hugged her knees and tucked the hem of her sleep shirt under her toes. She rocked and hummed "Old Man River" to keep her mind occupied and relax her enough to sleep.

It didn't work. She was afraid to go to sleep, afraid of the nightmare. Not the nightmare itself—she didn't remember those images—but its aftermath. Gus's getting upset and barking and that barking triggering the intercom to Gabe's room and Gabe's getting upset because she'd had the nightmare. It was too much. And she couldn't even turn off the intercom; the fancy contraption was hardwired to prevent it from being accidentally switched off.

"I'm going downstairs for ice cream, Gus. Come."

She unlocked the deadbolt on her door, and the two of them stole downstairs as the clock chimed a quarter after one. Nightlights lit the way to the kitchen, where she saw bright lights on. Gabe sat at the island, eating a bowl of ice cream.

"Looks like we had the same idea," Skye said.

Her brother smiled. "I'm missing Belle. We used to meet down here and eat ice cream together while she was staying here."

"When is she coming home?"

"Tomorrow afternoon. What's your problem? Sam?" He shoved a half-gallon carton of chocolate toward her, along with a spoon.

She peered inside and saw that not much was left, so she dug in without getting a bowl. "Not exactly. Just life in general. Gabe, do people think I'm weird? I mean, do they talk about it?"

He frowned. "What's this about, peanut? Did somebody say something to upset you?"

"Don't go all big brother on me, Gabe. I asked a simple question."

"Weird in what way?"

"Weird like Mother is weird. Fey. Different."

He grinned. "Mother is one of a kind. And everybody adores her for it, just like everybody adores you."

Skye tossed her spoon into the empty carton and stood. "I should have known that I wouldn't get a straight answer from you." She turned to leave.

"Whoa. Where did that come from? What's bothering you, Skye?"

"I'm just trying to look at myself objectively, trying to figure out how other people see me."

"People meaning Sam Outlaw?"

"Maybe. But not just Sam. You have to admit that I'm not an ordinary person with an ordinary life. And I'm tired of it. I'm ready for things to change."

"Change isn't always good," Gabe said.

"Maybe not, but it keeps life from being boring."

She went upstairs, determined to have a peaceful night's sleep. Just in case she did have the nightmare, she closed the door from her bedroom to her sitting room and slept on the couch to escape the intercom.

Despite her precautions, she awoke with Gabe kneeling beside her, bathing her face with a damp cloth.

"Shh," he said. "It's okay. You're safe. Let's get you to bed."

For a moment she didn't remember where she was, then things flooded back in. "How did you hear me?"

"The momma dog was having a barking fit."

She'd forgotten that Nana might rouse Gabe. She went to bed, relieved that, for that night, the dream was gone. But there was something different this time. She remembered glimpsing a face, and the image lingered along with the smell of pizza.

She didn't mention it to Gabe, but she did mention it to her therapist on the following Thursday afternoon.

"Let's try regression again," Barbara said. "But we'll go even more slowly this time. Anytime you begin to feel anxious, simply lift your index finger, and I'll back off and allow you to adjust."

They managed to make it through the morning of the abduction when she'd started her run to the point where Kaiser had yelped and gone down. After more relaxation suggestions, she recalled a sting in her hip, then nothing until she had a moment of arousal. She'd felt she was in a car, bound and blindfolded. The car had reeked of pizza. She'd tried to scream but found she was gagged as well. A man had told her to shut up, and he wouldn't hurt her. Then she remembered nothing until she awoke inside the box.

She became so agitated that Barbara quickly backed off and got her relaxed again, then brought her out of the trance.

"I never saw his face," Skye said.

"It doesn't seem like it. But now you know where the pizza smell comes in."

"Yes, and his voice sounded vaguely familiar."

"Someone you knew," Barbara said.

"Someone I knew," Skye echoed sadly. "But not well, I don't believe. Why do you think I get shadowy glimpses of his face in my nightmares?"

"I suspect that at an unconscious level you've made an association with his voice."

"Then why can't I *remember?*" Skye beat her fist against her thigh.

"Just be patient with yourself. When you're ready, it will come. How is your cue word working for you?"

"Very well, thanks."

They discussed her nightmares some more, and Barbara gave her some presleep suggestions on a CD that she thought would help make the dreams less frightening and more productive.

It seemed to work because that night she slept peacefully, and her first thought when she woke up was, *It's Friday!* She smiled and stretched and hopped out of bed.

Tonight it was dancing at Fancy's with Sam. What would she wear?

Something blue. He liked blue.

She hoped he hadn't forgotten. He hadn't called while he was in El Paso. Was that a bad sign?

The thought had barely left her head when her phone rang.

"Hey, doctor lady darlin'," Sam said. "I didn't wake you up, did I?"

"No, not at all. I was just thinking about you. Where are you?"

"In a hotel in El Paso. Things have been pretty crazy here all week, and I can't get a flight out until this afternoon. You still up for dancing tonight?"

"Sure, if you're up to it."

He laughed. "I think I can manage to dotter around the floor. How are the puppies doing?"

"They're doing great. Nana is being a terrific mother. And Pookie is happy as a clam, but I think she misses you. She goes to the front door and cocks her head as if she thinks you might come at any minute."

"Well, tell her I'll be there tonight about seven. Want to go out for some dinner first?"

"With Pookie?"

"No, darlin', with me."

"Sure."

"Then I'll see you tonight."

"Okay."

"Skye?"

"Yes?"

"I've missed you."

A tingle stole over her and she smiled. "I've missed you, too."

"DAMN," SAM MUTTERED when he hung up the phone. He'd meant to beg off their date. A caving buddy of his had asked him to stay over for a weekend trip to a newly discovered desert cave, but the minute he'd heard Skye's voice, and she'd said she'd been thinking about him, well…he couldn't get to Wimberley soon enough.

Despite his lectures to himself, he was falling head over heels for her. He spent the morning wrapping up his business in El Paso, packed his bags and headed for the airport, hoping he might catch an earlier flight home.

No such luck.

It was after five-thirty by the time Sam collected his bags and hot-footed it to his pickup in the long-term lot.

And then the damned thing wouldn't start. He ground and ground. And cussed and cussed. He finally flagged down a security car to give him a jump. Of all times for his battery to be dead.

He raced home, hopped in the shower and shaved. He dressed quickly, knowing he was cutting it close, and hurried back out to his truck, praying that it would start.

It didn't. The guy upstairs must have had other priorities. He pounded the steering wheel and let out several other choice expletives about the pickup's origin and character-istics. It didn't help. And to make matters worse, the damned horn got stuck. Inside the closed garage, the noise blasted his eardrums like a giant raspberry in retaliation for his curses.

Sod-pawing mad, he got out, threw up the hood and yanked loose a handful of wires. Thankfully, the noise stopped. But he was left without any transportation except his Harley, and he was running late.

He called Skye, and Suki answered.

"Suki, tell Skye I've had a delay, and I'm running late. I'm leaving San Antonio now. Bye."

He hadn't waited for an answer. He hopped on the motorcycle and roared off, wondering how Skye would react to his wheels. Better he found out now rather than later.

SKYE WAS WAITING IN the foyer when Ralph answered the door. Sam raked a hand through his hair as he stepped inside, his eyes on her, his grin wide.

"Hello, gorgeous," Sam said.

"Hello," Ralph answered in a deadpan.

Sam laughed. "Sorry, Ralph. I had my eyes on our girl here." He stuck out his hand to the big man. "How you been?"

"Just fine, thanks."

"Sorry I'm late," Sam said to Skye. "The battery in my pickup died. I hope Gabe doesn't mind driving again tonight."

"He probably wouldn't mind if he were here, but he and Belle had other plans tonight. They're not going to Fancy's."

"Oh." His smile died.

A small alarm went off inside her. "Is that a problem?"

"I can handle it if you can," he said. "You ready? I'm starving."

"I'm ready."

Ralph held open the door for them, and Sam put his hand to her back to guide her outside.

She looked around for a vehicle, but all she saw was a big black-and-chrome motorcycle. Panic started crawling up her throat. She must have said buttermilk to herself a dozen times before she said, "This is a motorcycle."

"I know," Sam said. "I rode it over here. Ever ridden a Harley?"

"Not that I recall."

He lifted an eyebrow. "You have a problem with it?"

Her breath caught when she looked up at him. She knew from the edge to his words that her answer was important, so she didn't hesitate. "No, not at all. I was just wondering where Gus would sit."

"Hmm. That is a problem. Think we could give him the night off?"

Skye did hesitate then. She didn't go anywhere without Gus.

"I'll wear my gun if it helps, and I swear to God, Skye, I won't let anything happen to you."

Buttermilk, buttermilk, buttermilk, buttermilk, buttermilk.

"I swear, Skye. Let's try it, and if you can't handle it, I'll bring you right home."

She swallowed. *Buttermilkbuttermilkbuttermilk.* She didn't trust her voice so she just nodded. She walked Gus back to the door, cleared her throat and said to Ralph, "Keep him here."

Ralph held Gus's collar. Gus whined, then started barking when Ralph closed the door. Skye clenched her teeth and strode back to Sam. "What do I do?"

He took an extra helmet from the pod on the back. "First put this on."

He helped her fasten it, then climbed on the big machine. "Get on behind me and hold on to my waist."

She'd sooner have climbed into a pit of rattlesnakes, but she repeated her mantra several times, threw her leg over the back and grabbed his waist like a spider monkey clinging to its mother.

He reached back, took her feet and placed them on two rests. "It'll be noisy, but I'll take it easy. Just relax."

Relax! *Ha! Buttermilk, buttermilk, buttermilk.*

He started the monster, and she must have jumped a foot. Her grip around his middle grew tighter. Her teeth were chattering, and they hadn't even moved yet. Thank heavens it was still light out or she really would have been terrified.

"Ready?" he yelled.

"Ready!"

They rode slowly down the drive to the guardhouse, but before he reached the gate, he turned the bike and headed back to the house.

"Where are you going?" she yelled.

"Back to the house. You're shaking like a leaf."

"It's because I'm excited." *Liar, liar. Buttermilk, buttermilk.* "I can do this. Let's go."

"Are you sure?"

"Yes."

He headed back toward the gate and waved at the guard as they exited.

"Buttermilk, buttermilk, buttermilk," she murmured.

"What?"

"Nothing," she yelled, forcing her shoulders to relax and pressing herself against Sam's back.

The worst of her terror ebbed, and as she became aware of her body and Sam's, a new set of feelings eased in. This was extremely…erotic. And quite…thrilling. She was reminded of the roller coasters she used to love as a kid. She also remembered how very close terror and sexual arousal were in brain function. By the time they reached the square a couple of minutes later, she was really getting into riding this monster.

Sam pulled to a stop and helped her off. She yanked off her helmet, fluffed her hair and grinned. "Wow!"

He laughed. "Wow, indeed. Did you like that?"

"I might get addicted, if you're not careful."

"I'll chance it. Hungry?"

"Famished," she said. "Are you in the mood for Tex-Mex?"

"Darlin', I'm always in the mood for Tex-Mex." He put their helmets in the pod and clipped his holster onto his belt.

He took her hand, and they walked across the street. She felt totally giddy, and she turned and walked backward, facing him. "That was really, really neat. Do you know that I've never been on a motorcycle before?"

"Nah," Sam said, feigning surprise. "I would have never guessed. Except you almost broke a couple of my ribs."

"Oh, dear. Did I hurt you?"

"No, goose. I'm teasing you."

They found a table and ordered margaritas while they studied the menu. Skye found herself frequently glancing to where Gus should be and feeling strange that he wasn't there. More than strange, she felt as if part of her was missing. She found herself imagining that he was there to relieve the building anxiety. The only place she ever went without him was to the bathroom, and he posted himself at the door until she came out.

"Are you okay?" Sam asked.

"I'm fine. What are you having?"

"Same thing I always have. Beef enchilada plate. How about you?"

"Black bean chalupas, I think."

A dog barked outside the front door. Skye glanced in that direction and saw Gus clawing on the glass panel.

"Is that Gus?" Sam asked.

Skye sighed and nodded.

Sam got up, went to the door and held it open. Gus shot inside and made straight for Skye.

"Hello, boy." She ruffled his scruff. "Where did you come from?"

Gus whined as if trying to answer and looked very pleased with himself.

When Sam sat down, Gus bared his teeth at him.

"Hey, don't blame me, buddy. There wasn't room for you on the bike."

"Gus, quiet."

Gus relaxed the snarl, but he sat at attention and kept his eye on Sam.

"You like enchiladas, Gus? I'll order you a plate."

"Sam! You wouldn't."

"I might if that would make him warm up to me."

Skye's cell phone rang, and she pulled it out of her pocket and answered. It was Suki, telling her that Gus had gotten out and was loose.

"Don't worry, Suki. Gus is here with me, and he can stay. I'll call when we're ready to leave Fancy's, and Ralph can pick him up."

When she hung up, Sam was frowning. "How did Gus find you so fast?"

Skye shrugged. "He's a good tracker."

"Like his daddy?"

"Mmm. Want some *queso?*"

WHEN THEY GOT TO FANCY'S, Sally and Tim Olds waved them over to join their table, and the four of them had a great time. Skye and Sam danced their feet off, then decided to call it an early night about ten-thirty.

While they waited for Ralph to come pick up Gus, Skye said, "You've had a busy day. Why don't you spend the night with us and avoid the long ride home tonight? I know Pookie is eager to see you."

"Don't tempt me, darlin', but I need to get my truck in running order as soon as possible. How about I come back tomorrow afternoon and pick up Pookie? Maybe we could catch a movie or something if you don't have any other plans."

"I have no plans, but Wimberley doesn't have any afternoon movies, and, anyhow, tomorrow is the first Saturday Market Day. The town will be teeming with people."

"Hey, I've heard about that, but I've never been. Belle said it's a blast. Maybe we could take it in."

Skye's stomach knotted up at the thought of being in the enormous crowd. "If you don't mind, I'm really not comfortable around such a mob."

"No problem. We'll think of something else."

"Bring your suit, and we can go for a swim."

"You're on," Sam said just as Ralph pulled up.

It took some doing, but Skye convinced Gus to ride with Ralph. She and Sam donned helmets and took off on the Harley. Skye wasn't nearly so nervous this time. She only said buttermilk about a half-dozen times. Actually, the open feeling of riding the bike was totally liberating. And she liked having her arms around Sam's muscled body. She felt completely safe with him. In fact, she was disappointed that they arrived home so quickly.

Gus had bounded from the SUV and met them as they pulled to a stop in front.

"Good boy," she said to the dog, kneeling and stroking him. "Would you like to come in, Sam?"

"I'd better get on the road, and you have work in the morning."

She stood, and they walked up the steps to the porch. "I had a wonderful time tonight, and I loved my first ride on a motorcycle."

"I'm glad." He caught her around the waist and kissed her. "I've been itching to do that all night."

"I've been itching for you to do it." She smiled and lifted her mouth again. Gus nudged between them.

The front door opened. "Sorry," Ralph said. "I was just turning off the alarm and unlocking the door for you. Go back to what you were doing." He beat a quick retreat.

Skye chuckled. "I think he was embarrassed."

"Ralph's a good guy. We'd better get you inside."

She didn't want to go inside alone. She would love to drag him along with her and jump his bones. Unfortunately, that was one of the down sides of living with your mother and brother and another couple. Reluctantly, she said good night and went inside.

Maybe she could convince him to spend the night tomorrow night. She could sneak into his room and…whatever. She smiled just thinking about all the possibilities.

Inside, she met her mother on the stairs. "Did you have a lovely time?" Flora asked.

"Yes, I did."

"Did you actually ride a *motorcycle?*"

Skye nodded.

"What fun! I haven't been on a motorcycle since Gabe was a baby, and we lived in a commune south of Houston. Isn't it delightfully freeing to zip along and feel the wind in your hair?"

"Yes, it is. Except that I wore a helmet. I was surprised that I enjoyed it. I thought I would be terrified. My therapy sessions are really helping."

Flora hugged her. "I'm so happy for you, dear. But I suspect that it's more than therapy sessions responsible for your emergence. I think Sam Outlaw has provided an impetus as well, and I adore him for that as well as lots of other reasons. I really must paint him. He's a fascinating man."

"He'll be back tomorrow. Maybe you can get him to sit for some more sketches then."

"We'll see. Good night, dear. Sleep well."

"Good night, Mom. Oh, how are Nana and the puppies?"

"Fine. I let Nana out to do her business earlier, and I've just been to check on them. It's amazing how a stray took to those helpless little things, though I'm rarely surprised at the way you have with animals."

Skye smiled. "It's my version of soul paintings."

EVEN THOUGH SAM WAS WORN OUT, he made a detour to one of the all-night superstores to pick up a battery for his truck. He would be that much ahead in the morning. Since he'd been gone for nearly a week, he also picked up some bread, eggs and milk for breakfast while he was at it. He never had gotten to be much of a cook, but he could handle scrambled eggs. He sometimes had them for both breakfast and supper—when he didn't hit the cafeteria a few blocks from him.

He wondered if Skye really couldn't cook. Not that it mattered. The kind of stuff she ate didn't require much finesse in the kitchen. He'd hate to know that he had to go the rest of his life without a rib eye or a big pot of chili—not that he had to be concerned about any long range plans with her. He still didn't see any kind of a future with her—except when he kissed her, and then he thought he'd like to hold her forever. But he couldn't afford her.

Still, she'd surprised the hell out of him when she'd climbed on the bike. Maybe he'd done it just to test her, figuring that she'd go ballistic over the idea—even worse than Julie used to. What had surprised him more, given that she'd obviously been nervous, was that she'd acted as though she'd really enjoyed it after she got used to it.

Now if he could just get her down in a cave...

He gave a wry laugh. Not a chance in hell. And no wonder. If he'd been buried alive like she had, he didn't figure that he'd be too anxious to go spelunking, either.

Chapter Thirteen

Changing the battery in his pickup didn't take much time, but reconnecting all the stuff he'd pulled loose when the horn went crazy was a little more tedious.

"Is Pookie home yet?" a small voice asked.

"Not yet, Kim," Sam told his young neighbor. "I'm going to bring her home tomorrow."

"Oh, good. I've missed her."

"I'm sure she missed you, too."

"Whatcha doing?"

"Trying to find where all these wires go so that my truck will run. Hand me that wrench, will you?"

"This little thing?"

"No, the bigger one next to it."

He tightened the last connection. "Now, let's see if it runs. Stand back, darlin', and let me try to start it."

It fired right up.

As soon as he got cleaned up and grabbed a burger at the drive-through, he figured that, by the time he got to Wimberley, Skye's family should be through with lunch—not that he was eager to see her or anything. Swear to God, he was getting like one of those animals she tended to. Give him long enough and he'd probably be following her around, panting.

Not smart, Sam. But then, when had he ever listened to logic where his heart was concerned?

At the gate, the guard waved him through. He'd learned the names of all the security force. This one was Pete. Wonder what Pete made as a guard? No matter. It was more than he could afford on his Ranger pay. Maybe if the oil wells they were drilling on Outlaw property in Naconiche came in, he'd have a lot more change in his pocket, but that was a maybe, and it still wouldn't provide the big bucks a security force cost.

He rang the bell and was surprised when Skye opened the door.

"That's a first," he said.

"What?"

"Your answering the door."

"I was expecting you, and I saw you through the peephole. I've got an emergency, and I need some help. Game?"

"Sure. What's up?"

"Bed Martens called. Sarabelle is very sick, and Bed's about driven himself crazy worrying about her. He's nearly ninety years old, and since she's too sick to walk, there's no way he can lift her. He just called begging me to help. I can't turn him down. Will you drive me?"

"Sure. Who or what is Sarabelle?"

"His pet pig."

"Pot bellied?"

"No. Yorkshire. She weighs four hundred pounds, and he's had her for years, since she was a piglet."

"Let's go," Sam said. He held open the door to his truck for Skye and Gus.

They stopped by the clinic for her to pick up some items, and she directed him toward the old man's place. When he glanced over at her, he noticed that she had a frown and was gnawing on her bottom lip.

"Something wrong?"

"I'm worried about Bed and Sarabelle. From the way he described her symptoms, it could be classical swine fever."

"Serious?"

"Very," she said. "It's also called hog cholera. It's almost always fatal. Losing Sarabelle would be devastating to Bed. She's all he's got."

"No family?"

"Not anymore. They've died out, but he's a tough old cedar chopper from way back."

"What's a cedar chopper?"

"The poor pioneers of this area had to cut cedars on their little bit of land to clear a place for farming or for livestock. They used cedar for fence posts or sold the posts for a little extra money. Soon some of the men had to grab their axes and chop cedar full time to eke out a living clearing land for other people."

"You mean those cedars?" Sam pointed to a bushy grove of small trees with shaggy, rough bark. "Hate those damned things. My nose runs like a son-of-a-gun every February from the pollen they put out. They're not good for anything except fence posts." He wiggled his nose just thinking about it. "And I was told that they're not even true cedars. They're junipers."

"Right. And cedar fever is a problem for a lot of people. Have you been to an allergist?"

"Yeah," Sam said. "Got some pills, but it still bothers me. Only thing I don't like about this part of the country."

"Turn left at that next bend," Skye said.

Sam pulled to a stop at what could only be called a shack, an unpainted place that couldn't have been more than two rooms, with a native stone chimney and a long porch on the front. A grizzled old man, rail-thin and in worn overalls and a gimme cap, sat in a roughly made rocking chair on the porch. A big white pig lay on the porch near his feet.

When they got out, Sam didn't have to ask what the symptoms of swine fever were. The stench hit him like a wrecking ball, and the evidence of Sarabelle's messes covered the porch. Even Gus seemed reluctant to approach. He hung back a little, but Skye didn't even wrinkle her nose.

She just smiled and said, "Afternoon, Bed. Sorry that Sarabelle is ailing." She shook hands with the old man, then introduced Sam to Mr. Bedford Martens. "Sam's a good friend of mine."

Sam tugged at the front of his hat brim and shook hands.

"A Texas Ranger, I see from your badge," Bed said. "Good man to have around. Sarabelle took to grunting during the night, and her bowels started running off this mornin'. She's been just laying around, not her usual self. I'm fearful of cholera."

Skye nodded, then squatted to examine the Yorkshire while Gus took up his post at the foot of the steps.

"She doesn't have any fever," Skye said. "That's a good sign. I'll take a sample to check, but I think we can rule out cholera."

"Thank the good Lord," Bed said. "You hear that, Sarabelle? I was afraid you was a goner for sure." He patted the sow's rump, and she grunted.

Skye worked on the pig, but when she brought out the needles, Sam turned his attention away from her treatment. He didn't care much for needles. An old pickup under a tree caught his eye. No two panels were the same color, except for the rust spots, and the vehicle must have been at least thirty years old. It looked as if it were held together with determination and baling wire.

"That truck looks like a classic," Sam said to the old man.

Bed nodded. "Not as purdy as it was new, but it runs as good as the day I bought it. Except when it don't."

"Bed," Skye said, "I've given Sarabelle a shot for her diarrhea. She may just have some sort of virus, or it may be something else. We'll watch her and see how she does. I'll check on her tomorrow. Tell me, has she had any change in her diet in the past couple of days?"

Bed rubbed the prickly white whiskers of his chin. "Can't say that she has. Last night after supper we shared a beer and a candy bar like we do most nights. Now, missy, don't go jumping on me about that. I didn't give her but a sip or two of the beer, but she ate a right smart bite of that candy bar. It's a new kind I got that don't have no sugar in it. She liked it real good and begged so, that I gave her another one."

Skye's eyebrow went up. "Do you still have the wrapper from the candy?"

"'Spect I do." Bed rose and went into the house.

He came back with two crumpled wrappers from giant-sized chocolate bars and handed them to Skye. She smoothed out one of the papers and read the ingredients.

"Bed," she said, "Looks like this may be the culprit. Instead of sugar, the manufacturer uses a substitute that can cause digestive problems. See right here in small print, it says that an excess of this product can cause cramping and diarrhea. Don't give her any more of this. If you think she needs something sweet, give her an apple. It's better for her."

"Well, I'll be switched," the old man said. "I didn't see that part. My eyes ain't as good as they used to be."

"I think she'll be fine, but I'll check back tomorrow to be sure," Skye said.

"You sure took a load off my mind, I tell you," the old man said. "Wait here just a minute. I got something to show my thanks."

He came back with a gallon ice-cream carton full of black-berries and a little wooden flower that he gave to Skye. Sam took the berries.

"Thank you, Bed," Skye said. "This is beautiful. And we'll use the berries for a cobbler tonight."

"I'm much obliged to you, little lady. My regards to your mama."

When they got to his pickup, Sam wiped his feet on the grass before he got in, and he noticed that Skye discreetly did the same. Now he understood why she wore a pair of rubber clogs.

After they drove away, Sam hooted with laughter. "Chocolate candy and beer. Can you believe it? He's a character."

"Yes, he is. But he loves Sarabelle."

"The old fellow needs to get some glasses."

"Wouldn't do any good," Skye said. "He can see fine. He just can't read."

"How does he get by? He's obviously not in any shape to clear land these days."

"He has chickens and a milk cow and he raises a few goats. He has a couple of fruit trees, and he plants a garden every year and puts up food from his patch. He barters milk and eggs or sells them. And he whittles."

"Whittles?"

She held out the delicate flower he'd given her. "He made this, and he made the rocking chair he sits in. I have one in my room. He sells those for a little extra money to live on. With the help of local agencies and neighbors, he gets by."

"And you get blackberries and a doodad for your fee."

"Sometimes I get eggs or buttermilk."

"You must like buttermilk."

"Why?" she asked.

"I hear you muttering it all the time."

She laughed. "It's a word that my therapist gave me to relax."

"Does it work?"

"Surprisingly well. Which reminds me, I didn't get an opportunity to tell you about it last night. She did another regression with me on Thursday and plans another tomorrow."

"Oh?" He clamped his teeth to keep from saying more. Granted, Fancy's wasn't an ideal place for conversation, but she'd had plenty of opportunity to tell him during dinner the night before. But she hadn't. Why?

"It's the strangest thing. I still can't remember much, but I recalled being in his car that day, and it smelled of pizza. That's probably why I can't stand pizza anymore, and I used to practically live on the stuff."

"Hmm."

"Go ahead," Skye said, "I know you're itching to ask me more."

"I was just trying to think why his car smelled like pizza, then I remembered that probably half the college kids' cars in America smell of pizza. I remember that we used to eat it at least three times a week. Or more."

"So did my roommate and I when we were in veterinary school. Especially at exam time. But we had it delivered."

They glanced at each other.

"Oh, my God," Skye said quietly. "It could have been the delivery guy."

"Do you remember his name or what he looked like?"

She shook her head. "Not his name. I vaguely recall that he was lanky and dark haired. Lisa might remember more."

"Who's Lisa? Gabe's former fiancée?"

"No, different Lisa. Lisa Williams was my roommate. She's a veterinarian in San Antonio now."

"What was the name of the pizza place?"

"Zelda's. Odd name for a pizza parlor, I know, but it had been there forever and was very popular with the students at College Station."

"Not so odd if the owner's name was Zelda."

"But it wasn't. I think the original owner was named Jimmy, and he was an English major who had a thing for Fitz-gerald."

"Is it still around?"

"I don't have the slightest idea, but I can find out easily enough." Skye pulled out her cell phone, dialed and asked for Zelda's Pizza in College Station, Texas. After a few seconds, she said, "It's ringing. Oh, hello. I was just wondering if you were still doing business." She laughed, then said, "Thanks."

"I presume that they're open?"

"'Still going strong,' they said. 'And serving the best pizza in Texas.'"

"It's a start," Sam said. "Mind calling Lisa to see if she remembers the name of your delivery guy?"

"Not at all." Skye used her cell phone again, but she left a message asking her friend to call her. "I got her voice mail. You ready to go swimming?"

"I am. Actually, I'm more interested in seeing you in that little bitty bathing suit of yours." He winked. "Are we going to have chaperones this afternoon?"

"Maybe. Gabe and Belle might join us if they get back from Austin in time. They were having lunch with one of Gabe's clients."

Sam loved his sister, and Gabe was his best friend, but he hoped to hell that they decided to go to a movie or something.

THE MINUTE THEY OPENED the door, Pookie came running to Sam. Tiger ran after her. Pookie started yapping to beat the band.

"What's wrong, girl?" he asked.

"She's scolding you," Skye said. "I think she was worried about your being gone so long. And she didn't even get to see you yesterday when you picked me up."

Sam dropped his bag and scooped up the little dog. "Sorry, Pookie. I didn't figure that you'd miss me."

"She's very attached to you," Skye said.

Pookie continued to alternately yip and lick Sam's chin. "Come on, girl," he said, "let's go put on our bathing suits and talk about it. Not on the mouth, Pookie. Not on the mouth."

Chapter Fourteen

Skye had just slipped on her suit when her cell phone rang.

"What's up, roomie?" Lisa Williams asked. "I haven't heard from you in a coon's age. Sorry I missed your call. I was out stocking the larder."

"No problem. I was hoping that you were out with some gorgeous guy."

"I wish. How's your love life?"

"Looking up," Skye said. "We're just about to go swimming."

"What does he look like in a bathing suit?"

"Like you wouldn't believe. Six-and-a-half feet of lovely muscle and gorgeous."

"Then why are you talking to me?"

Skye laughed. "Good question. Actually, I wanted to ask you something. Do you remember the guy who used to deliver us pizza from Zelda's?"

"Vaguely. Kind of lanky. Dark hair. He always creeped me out."

"Did he? Why?"

"Lord, I don't know. It's been too many years. Why on earth are you asking about him?"

"Do you remember his name?" Skye asked.

"Uh-h-h-h…wait a minute. Wait a minute. Dennis. That

was it. I always thought of Dennis the Menace. What is this about?"

At the sound of his name, his face flashed like a quick snapshot, and a chill went over Skye, and the smell of pizza almost overpowered her. She felt her hand tremble as she held the phone and fought to keep a tremor from her voice. "I'm trying to dredge up memories of my abduction, but there are lots of blanks during that period."

"Skye, my God! You don't think it was Dennis who kidnapped you?"

"I don't know, Lisa. I just don't know. It may be nothing. I may be grasping at straws. Listen, I've gotta go. Thanks for your help."

"Whoa, girlfriend. Don't leave me hanging. Call me later and tell me what's going on. We have lots to catch up on."

"I will. Bye."

Skye was still trembling when she hung up. Dennis. Was he the one? Her stomach heaved, and she ran for the bathroom.

SAM LAY POOLSIDE, stretched out on a chaise with Pookie resting on his belly. He'd been waiting for a while and was about to give up and go check on Skye when she came out the back door with Gus. His impatience disappeared, and he was hit with instant arousal. The bikini she wore was a killer. It was blue, and it hugged every curve like a lover. She was heaven on a plate, and his eyes feasted on her from the pink tips of her toes, up her long, lovely legs, over her hips and breasts, then stopped as he saw the expression on her face.

"What's wrong?" he asked.

The feeble smile she returned was as phony as a three-dollar bill. "Nothing's wrong."

"Don't ever try to rob a bank, darlin'."

"What you mean?"

"You don't lie worth a damn. You're as pale as a lifer. You look like you've seen a ghost."

"Maybe I have." She tossed a towel over a chair back, walked to the apron of the pool and dived in.

Sam dived in after her, but she swam like an otter, surfacing and diving and alluding him when he reached for her. He finally caught her in chest-high water and pulled her against him.

"What kinds of ghosts have you been seeing?"

"The spooky kind," she said, locking her arms around his neck and pulling his head down to kiss him.

A kiss wasn't enough. If it hadn't been broad daylight and her mother and God knows who else hadn't been in the house, he would have stripped that little blue scrap off her and—

"Are we interrupting?"

Sam looked up to see Gabe and Belle, in swimsuits and headed to the pool.

"Damned right you are." He could have cheerfully throttled his sister.

Skye splashed him. "Oh, Sam!" She darted away. "Come on in. The water's glorious today." She surface-dived and disappeared.

Belle dived in and started doing laps.

Sam lifted himself onto the apron, then stood and slicked back his hair. "How's it going, Gabe?"

"Can't complain. Were you just kissing my sister?"

"I was. Haven't you been kissing mine?"

"I have." Gabe handed Sam a towel. "Want a beer?"

"Sure."

Gabe opened the cooler he'd brought out and handed him an icy can. Sam popped the top, took a long swig. "Skye's upset about something. I was just about to get it out of her when you two showed up."

Gabe lifted his eyebrows. "Interesting form of interrogation."

"Bug off, Gabe. We've had this conversation before."

"Yeah, I guess we have." He opened a beer and sat down

at an umbrella table. "Mother said you went with Skye on a house call. That's rare for her."

"She had an emergency with a pig." Sam related the story of Bed and Sarabelle, embellishing it as the tale unfolded until Gabe hooted with laughter.

"What's so funny?" Belle asked as she walked toward them, wringing out her hair. "Guy jokes?" She took Gabe's beer, sipped from it, then handed it back.

"No," Gabe said, "but we're going to have to get Sam some rubber boots before he makes another house call with Skye." He let out another whoop of laughter.

SKYE ENJOYED SPENDING THE afternoon and evening with Gabe and Belle. She really did. She even relented, and she and Sam went to the outdoor movie with them, and she hadn't been in years. They all took lawn chairs—as everybody did—to watch a film that was touted to be a contender for an Oscar. She felt totally secure with Gus at her feet, Gabe sitting on one side and Sam on the other and with people she knew all around her, but what she'd wanted was to spend some time alone with Sam.

Wouldn't it be great to have a townhouse like Belle? When Gabe took Belle home tonight, he wouldn't drop her off at the door with a chaste kiss. They would go inside where it was private. She'd been thinking a lot about privacy lately.

And a lot of other things. Like driving. She was going to look into getting her driver's license renewed and take a few practice runs around the grounds to see if she was still competent to drive. She got a little antsy when she thought about driving anywhere alone, but she and Belle were starting karate lessons next Thursday morning. With her therapy sessions and learning self-defense tactics, she should be okay with short trips around Wimberley. She could certainly make it to the clinic and back without having Napoleon there. And there was always Gus. Gus would protect her with his life.

But then Kaiser hadn't been able to protect her. She shuddered and shook off the memory.

"Cold?" Sam whispered.

She shook her head. "I'm fine." He put his arm around her shoulders anyhow, and she didn't complain.

When the movie was over, Sam stood and stretched, then folded his and Skye's lawn chairs. "Good movie. I've been to drive-ins before, but this is the first time I've ever been to a walk-in."

"I'd suggest stopping somewhere for a drink," Gabe said, "but with this being Market Day, most of the places will still be crowded. The Walker-Burrell place has a well-stocked bar."

"Sounds good to me," Sam said.

"And to me," Belle added.

Sounded terrible to Skye, who was still thinking about some alone time with Sam, but she said, "Me, too."

After they arrived home, Flora, Ralph and Suki were still up watching TV, and Gabe fixed nightcaps for everybody. It seemed as if Gabe and Belle practically gulped theirs down. Then Gabe announced that he was driving Belle home. Skye hid a smile. Looked like somebody else was eager for alone time.

As soon as Belle and her brother left, her mother, Ralph and Suki scattered as well. Tiger went upstairs with Flora, but Pookie wouldn't budge from Sam's lap. Even when he put the little dog down to move to the couch beside Skye, Pookie scrambled up to plant herself back in the space she'd staked out.

"Do you ever feel as if the world is conspiring to keep us from having some time alone?" Sam asked.

"I've been thinking that all day."

"I've been thinking about this all day." He lifted her chin and kissed her.

His lips felt wonderful against hers, and she touched her tongue to his.

He pulled her closer, and stroked a slow, strong hand up the side of her thigh, over her hip, around her abdomen and under her T-shirt to her breast.

She moaned with pleasure.

Gus growled.

"Ignore him," she murmured against Sam's lips. She moaned again as his thumb slowly circled her nipple.

Gus growled again, and Pookie started yipping.

"He's hard to ignore when he's chewing on my second-best pair of jeans."

"Gus! Release!" She leaned her forehead against Sam's. "This would be funny if it weren't so frustrating. I'm sorry about the jeans."

"Maybe we could put him outside."

She sighed. "He'd only bark until we let him back in."

"Does he go *every place* with you?"

"Yep. Except to the bathroom. Then he stands guard at the door. I like to bathe in privacy."

They looked at each other and grinned.

"It's worth a try," he said, and they hurried upstairs to her room.

She flung open the bathroom door. "Oops. I forgot. Nana and her pups are in here."

"Can't you move them?"

Skye looked at him and rolled her eyes.

Sam heaved a big sigh. "Guess not. Want to try my digs?"

They hurried to the guest suite. Gus and Pookie trotted after them, rather Gus trotted. Pookie scampered in circles around them, yipping.

Sam scooped up the little dog. "Hush, Pookie, or I'm going to send you to the dog meat factory."

She gave another tiny yip and licked his chin.

Inside the suite, Sam locked the door and put Pookie on the couch. "Stay there and be quiet."

Pookie cocked her head as Sam talked to her, her tiny

tongue hanging out and her bottom twitching. The moment he turned to leave, Pookie jumped down and scampered after him.

Skye chuckled. "I think she needs some obedience training."

"You think it would help?"

"Of course."

"I'll check out classes first thing Monday morning." He threw his arm around Skye and headed for the bathroom.

Skye gave Gus a hand signal at the door, and Sam set Pookie beside the shepherd with a command to stay. Pookie cocked her head again and gave him a doggy smile.

The second the door to the bathroom closed, Gus started growling and Pookie began yipping and scratching on the door.

"Ignore them," Skye said as Sam pulled her close for a kiss.

"I can ignore them easily enough, but what about your mother?"

"My mother was a flower child. She's very open-minded."

As their lips met, the yipping and scratching grew louder, and a bloodcurdling yowl reverberated from the bedroom.

"What the hell is that?" Sam asked.

"The Siamese must have been hiding under your bed. They can be very noisy when they're agitated."

Gus started barking, Sam cursed and their romantic interlude was lost.

"Babe," Sam said, "this doesn't seem to be working out."

"I'm sorry."

"Not your fault, but it's frustrating as hell." He kissed her nose and opened the door. He could have sworn that those damned dogs grinned at him. "Next weekend," he said to Pookie, "you're staying home."

"And you and I," Skye said to Gus, "are going to have some sessions in privacy training."

Chapter Fifteen

Skye hugged her pillow and turned over in bed. She was beyond frustrated, and sleep was out of the question. She'd never thought she would begrudge having Gus by her side every minute, but right now she wished for a night of privacy. Even an hour would do. But Gus was only doing what he had been trained to do: stay by her side and protect her. She couldn't scold him for that.

Sometimes at the clinic, when she was seeing an animal that would be disturbed by Gus's presence, she put Gus in a crate in the back, and he handled it very well. She was tempted to take him over to the clinic and put him in the crate for a few minutes, then sneak into Sam's room. But that would require going out alone. At night. In the dark. She wasn't that brave yet. And she wasn't about to ask anyone to go with her. She'd be too embarrassed. Anyhow, everybody was already asleep.

And there was still Pookie to contend with.

Next weekend, he'd said, he was leaving Pookie at home. So he planned to come back. She wondered about that. She wondered about Sam's feelings for her a lot. He didn't seem to be the type of man to tie himself to a neurotic woman—not that he wasn't the sweetest, kindest man in the world. He was. He was very patient and understanding, but she couldn't help but worry if he wasn't hanging around just to get a lead on the kidnapping cases.

Surely not. That would break her heart.

Maybe that was the reason that she hadn't told Sam about Lisa's call. She didn't want to put the possibility to the test. She'd have to tell him about Dennis sooner or later. But she would wait. She wanted to be very sure before she said anything.

And she wanted to be stronger. She used to be confident and fearless. No, she didn't *used to be*, she still was. Under all the garbage, she was still the same person—older and wiser and more experienced for sure, but the same person. By damn, she was going to reclaim that part of herself. Some pizza-delivering creep wasn't going to rob her of a life. She was going to confront her demons once and for all.

Enough already! Enough!

THE FOLLOWING MORNING after breakfast, Sam took Skye and Gus up in the hills to check on Bed and Sarabelle. They found the pair sitting on the front porch. The pig seemed fine, and the porch was freshly scrubbed and smelled of bleach.

"She acts like her old self this mornin'," Bed said. "Things seemed to turn around after you left. I throwed the last bar of that candy away. I'm much obliged to you, Dr. Skye."

Skye handed him a bag of apples she'd pilfered from the pantry. "These will be better as treats for her."

"Thank you, kindly. How was that cobbler?"

"Best I've ever had, Bed. Thanks. And Mama sends her thanks as well."

The old man nodded.

"I liked that cobbler, too," Sam said, handing Bed the empty ice-cream carton the berries had been in.

"There's plenty more of them berries down by the fence, if you want to pick another gallon."

Skye glanced at Sam as they got into his truck. "Want to pick berries?"

"Sure, but I need to get going pretty soon. I've got to grocery-stop and do my laundry."

"Do you really do your own laundry?"

"I do if I want clean clothes. I send my suits and dress shirts to the cleaners, but I do everything else. If I don't wash stuff, I'll be down to my holey underwear."

Skye laughed. "Only you would say that."

"It's the truth. I've been gone for a week, and things have piled up. I've got a stack of mail that would choke a horse, most of them bills I need to pay. Where are those berries?"

They found the vines along a fence line and filled the carton in no time.

"I haven't been berry-picking in a long time," Sam said, tossing a handful of the juicy morsels in his mouth and feeding a couple to Skye. "All us kids used to pick berries every year, and we usually ate more than we picked. Mama would make jelly out of some of them and put the rest in the freezer for pies. Brings back memories." He ate another handful.

"Do you miss Naconiche?"

"Not really. I visit quite a bit, but, like Belle, I can't see myself living there. I'd just be the youngest Outlaw boy to my three brothers. I like being a Texas Ranger. It's what I dreamed of since I was just a kid. And I feel really good about being a part of the Unsolved Crimes Investigation Team."

Skye felt herself tense, thinking that he might mention her case. He didn't. They carried the berries back to the truck, and Sam found some packets of hand wipes in the console. He took her hands and wiped the berry juice from them. It felt very…intimate.

"Is your tongue purple?" he asked.

She stuck it out.

"Bright purple." He leaned over and kissed her. "But you taste good, better than cobbler."

Gus growled.

"Shut up, Gus," Sam said. He kissed her again.

She was very careful not to moan.

"ARE THINGS GETTING SERIOUS between you and Sam?" Gabe asked as they drove to Austin for her Sunday afternoon therapy session.

"Serious in what way?"

"Serious in the usual way. Are you falling in love with him?"

She didn't answer right away, mostly because she didn't know the answer. Was she?

"I like Sam a lot. He's a very attractive man and a super nice guy, but love? I think it's too soon to tell."

"Be careful, Skye. Don't let him break your heart."

"In the first place, what makes you think he would? I just might break his. But, frankly, I don't think anybody will end up with a broken heart. I'm learning to live again, Gabe, and Sam is helping me. I'm not looking beyond that. For now we're having a wonderful time together. Please don't spoil it for me."

Gabe opened his mouth to say more, then closed it. "You think this therapist is helping you?"

"Immensely. Gabe, I want to start driving again, and I'm sure my license has lapsed. How do I go about getting it reinstated?"

"As far as I know, it's current. I renewed it on-line a few months ago, and it's good for another six years."

"Great! Will you ride with me around the grounds this afternoon to see if I still remember how to drive?"

"Sure."

Skye gave a contented sigh. "You can't imagine how fantastic the idea of driving again makes me feel. I'm done with still being held captive by that low-life who abducted me."

"Sic 'em, tiger."

She felt almost giddy with excitement, and her good mood

carried into her therapy session, which was extremely productive. With the help of hypnosis, she was able to confront
Dennis, the pizza man. And it *was* him. She was sure of it. His
face became very clear, and Barbara led her through an
exercise to confront him and her fears and confirm that she
was reclaiming her power.

With she came out of the trance, she laughed. "I feel like
singing!"

Barbara smiled. "Do it."

Skye jumped up, shoved her fist in the air and started
singing "I've Got the Power" and dancing around.

Barbara clapped and sang along with her.

Skye collapsed into her chair, grinning from ear to ear.
"God, that felt good."

"Make it your mantra," Barbara said. "Does thinking of
Dennis make you afraid?"

Skye stopped for a minute and brought his face into focus.
There was emotion connected to his image, but it had changed.
"It's not fear I feel. It's anger. Fury. I'd like to castrate the son
of a bitch for what he did to me and to all those other women.
Castrate him with a rusty knife."

"Wow, that's a change."

"Isn't it? I can't tell you how much I appreciate what
you've done for me, Barbara. You've given me back my life."

"No, you've taken back your life yourself. You were
ready—and motivated. I merely facilitated."

Skye hugged her. "Whatever you did, I appreciate it. Now
I can give Sam and the Texas Ranger team the information
they need to find the bastard."

"HE SORT OF REMINDS ME of that tall guy in *O Brother, Where
Art Thou*," Skye told her mother at they sat in Flora's studio
that night.

"You mean George Clooney?"

"No, no, the other tall guy, the one that turned into a frog."

"Well, dear, he didn't actually turn into a frog. They only thought he did."

"I know, Mom. Pete, that was the character's name. His real name is John Turturro. I checked it on the Internet. Do you remember him?"

"Very well. He was so funny. I loved that movie. I always wondered why you didn't. Now I know. Pete reminded you of that terrible man."

"Dennis. Yes, he did. I just didn't understand it at the time. He looked sort of like a cross between Turturro and Jerry Seinfeld, except his ears stuck out. His nose was definitely Seinfeld. And his hair. Dark and very curly."

Flora began to make quick strokes on her pad and shivered as she did so. "He's an evil, evil man."

As Skye visualized him and described the image, her mother drew an exact likeness of the kidnapper. "His ears were a little bigger, and his eyebrows fuller. That's it."

"Perfect," Skye said when her mother finished. "Perfect. You captured him precisely. Mom, you're a genius." She hugged her mother and grabbed the sketch. "I'm going to go call Sam right now."

Flora glanced at her watch. "Dear, it's after ten o'clock. Isn't it a little late to call?"

"Maybe, but I'm going to do it anyhow. The sooner Sam gets on the case, the sooner this cretin will be caught and put away."

"Will you feel safe then, Skye?"

Skye, startled by her mother's question, thought about it for a moment. "I don't know. Maybe. Or I may have to battle fear for a long time before I conquer it completely. In any case, this is important. Just think of all those young women who were never found."

In her sitting room, Skye curled up on the couch and phoned Sam. He answered "Outlaw" on the second ring.

"Outlaw? Sam Outlaw, the famous Texas Ranger?"

He chuckled. "I don't know how famous I am."

"You might be. Guess what I'm holding in my hand this very instant?"

"Kryptonite."

"Nope."

"Blackberry cobbler."

She laughed. "No, something even better. A sketch that my mother made of my kidnapper. His name is Dennis. And he did deliver pizza from Zelda's when Lisa and I were in veterinary school."

"Skye, that's amazing. How did you put all that together?"

She told him about Lisa's call and about her therapy session that afternoon. "It's a very good sketch, Sam, and I'm sure it will help you track him down."

"Do you mind if I drop by tomorrow and pick it up? I'll buy you lunch."

"You don't have to buy my lunch. We always have a feast here. Join us."

"I was thinking of something a little more private."

"Were you now?" She smiled. "Come by the clinic at twelve, and I'll have Maria pack us a picnic lunch."

"You're on. I'll be there."

MONDAY MORNINGS WERE ALWAYS hectic, which was just as well. She didn't have as much time to watch the clock, waiting for noon and Sam's arrival. He rang the bell just as Napoleon and the morning receptionist were leaving for lunch.

He looked marvelous in a gray western-cut suit and blue tie. He held his signature Ranger's white cowboy hat and smiled when he saw her.

"My, don't you look fine," Skye said. "I feel like a slouch up beside you."

"You don't look like a slouch to me." He gave her a quick kiss. "You look ready for a picnic. And my stomach's ready, too. I spoke at a breakfast meeting of a men's club this morning, and everybody ate breakfast except me."

"Poor baby. Let me wash up, and we'll be on our way."

"Where are we going?"

"Not far. It's a surprise."

Skye stowed her lab coat, fluffed her hair and washed her hands. After applying a touch of lip gloss, she grabbed her bag with her cell phone, keys and the remote. The picnic basket was already waiting on the receptionist's counter.

"Ready?" she asked.

"Darlin', I was born ready."

Laughing, she kissed his cheek. "You, Sam Outlaw, are a mess." She handed him the basket while she locked up.

"What's in here?" he asked, lifting one corner of the lid while she locked up.

"Tofu and mung bean sprouts."

He made a face. "Tell me you're kidding."

"Bean sprouts are good for you."

"That's what my mama used to tell me about liver."

"And you were a hard sell."

"You got that right."

Sam opened the passenger door for Skye, and Gus hopped into the backseat in his usual place. "Can we trust him with the basket?"

"Of course."

Sam stowed their lunch in the back beside Gus, and climbed into the driver's seat. "Where to?"

"Not far. Go out the front gate and turn left." They waved to the guard as they passed and turned onto the road. "Now take the first left."

"Here?" Sam asked, pulling to a stop at an iron gate with big Private Property and No Trespassing signs prominently displayed. "Have you got a key?"

"Nope, but I have this." She pulled the remote from her bag, punched it, and the gate swung open.

"Who does this belong to?"

"Gabe. And me, I guess. He gave me half interest for my

twenty-first birthday. It's part of the main property, but it's too hard to fence securely, so it's kept separate. Just follow the road to the river."

The trees grew thicker as they wound through the river property. Fond memories drifted into her thoughts as they pulled to a stop in a shady grove near the picnic tables. She got out and walked to the bank while Sam shucked his coat and tie to leave in the seat and carried the basket to one of the concrete tables. She breathed in the familiar fecund scent of the area and listened to the birds in the trees and the ripple of water over the rocky bed. A prickle of chill bumps rushed over her. The good kind.

He stood behind and wrapped his arms around her. "It's beautiful here."

"Isn't it? I've always loved this place. I practically lived here every summer before—before I was abducted. When I was a kid, I had a rope on that tree over there, tied so my friends and I could swing out and splash into the water. I haven't been here in years."

"Feel good about coming now? Feel safe with me?"

"I feel wonderful. I've missed it. And I feel perfectly safe with you."

"Looks like a good spot for canoeing or kayaking," Sam said.

"It is. Want to go canoeing next weekend?"

"Sounds great."

Sam's stomach growled, and Skye chuckled. "Sorry. I forgot that you're starving. Let's eat our tofu sandwiches now."

"Good idea. My stomach's about stuck to my backbone as my daddy would say."

They walked back to the table, and Skye opened the big basket. "Manuel cleaned the table this morning, so your nice pants should be safe." She took a large cardboard folder from on top and handed it to him. "Dennis," she said simply, then proceeded to unload the food.

She watched from the corner of her eye as he opened the folder and studied her mother's sketch.

"Sorry son of a bitch," he muttered. "So that's him. You know, he kind of reminds me of that actor, what's-his-name, that was one of George Clooney's sidekicks in *O Brother, Where Art Thou*. Did you see that?"

"Yes. His name is John Turturro, and he played Pete, the tall one."

"But the nose is different. And the ears. And, of course, the hair. As I recall, Pete didn't have much hair. You're sure his name was Dennis?"

"Lisa said so, and I'm pretty sure that's right. Mom made copies and added various kinds of facial hair and so forth."

He glanced at the other pictures. "Fantastic. Flora is a genius." He took her hand and brought it to his mouth. "Thanks, Skye. I know this has been hard for you. We'll get right on it." He set the folder aside. "Now bring on the tofu."

She opened a foil-wrapped package and looked inside. "Yum. This is an avocado and jicama sandwich with walnuts, sunflower seeds and alfalfa sprouts. Try it." She held out half to him.

He looked at it as if it were toasted grasshoppers, then took a chomp. He chewed and swallowed. "You know, that's not half-bad."

"Told you," she said. "But here's a roast beef if you'd rather have that."

"Believe I would. Not that the avocado wasn't good, but I'm sure you'd rather have that one." He grinned.

She set out potato salad and sliced cantaloupe and poured iced tea from a thermos. In no time, Sam had put away two roast beef sandwiches, the rest of the avocado half he'd tasted and had scraped the potato salad bowl. She'd had one piece of melon, and he'd demolished the rest.

"Any berry cobbler in there?" he asked, peeking into the basket.

"No, but there's chocolate cake."

"Whoo-wee, that's my favorite."

"Sam, everything is your favorite."

"Not everything. I don't like liver or turnips. And I can live without cauliflower." As she brought out the cake, he pulled her into his lap. "I'd even pass up chocolate cake if I could make out a little with you."

"Oh, really?"

"Really."

He kissed her, and it felt so warm and soft and wonderful that she forgot to be quiet. His hand moved under her shirt to cup her breast and she moaned again.

Gus growled.

"Down, boy," she said.

"Who? Me or Gus?"

"Gus. You're doing fine." She brushed her lips across his and pressed against his hand.

"I can't afford for him to ruin these pants. This is one of my best suits."

"Then we'd better eat our cake."

"I don't know, darlin'. I might risk the suit for another kiss."

She was seriously considering offering to buy him another suit when a series of catcalls and laughter rang out from the river. A boat full of teenagers and another filled with a family rowed past them.

Sam reluctantly moved his hand, and she rose. "Am I beginning to feel a little paranoid?" she asked. "Or do you think the powers that be are conspiring against us?"

"What say that next weekend we lock up the dogs and go to a motel?"

"I think that's a brilliant idea."

Chapter Sixteen

Skye mopped her face and slipped into her flip-flops. "I'm sure glad I had yoga classes first," she said to Belle and Sally, "or I would have been in no shape for this."

"I hear that," Sally said.

Both wearing the traditional pants and jacket uniform of karate, they sat down to watch Belle work out with the advanced instructor. Skye and Sally had just had their semi-private karate lesson, and they were ahead of the game because of the intro instructions from Belle. At least they already knew how to tie their white belts. Belle's was black.

Gus sat at Skye's feet, and she kept a finger in his collar to keep him from jumping to Belle's defense.

"Gus doesn't get it," she told Sally. "I'm going to have to leave him at home next week. Watching me yell and punch will have him in a frenzy."

"I thought you didn't go anywhere without Gus," Sally said.

"I usually don't, but having him with me all the time is giving me some grief lately. For some reason, Sam isn't one of his favorite people, and I don't understand why."

"I do," Sally said. "Gus is a male, isn't he? He's jealous."

Skye chuckled. "You may be right, but I suspect that he's just being overly protective. I've been retraining him."

"To do what?"

"To stay at home or in the kennel without barking or trying to escape and follow me."

"Is it working?"

"I hope so. Sam is running out of jeans."

Sally cocked an eyebrow. "Sounds interesting. There must be a story there."

"Let's just say that Gus doesn't like it when Sam kisses me. I think he misinterprets."

"Who? Sam or Gus?" Sally asked, a devilish gleam in her eyes.

"Enough said about the subject. Isn't Belle fascinating to watch? Wonder if we'll ever be that good?"

"Dream on, girlfriend. Are you really learning to shoot a gun?"

Skye nodded. "Belle finally talked me into it. We went to the shooting range last night. It was ladies' night. You should come with us next week. It's kind of fun. The Culbertson twins were there, too. I figure if two old ladies can learn, so can I."

"I already have a license to carry," Sally said.

"Carry what?"

"A gun. I have one in my purse right now."

"You're kidding."

"Nope," Sally said. "This is Texas, sweetie. I grew up around guns, and my daddy insisted that I understand gun use and safety."

"I guess I've led a sheltered life. I don't think there was ever a gun in our house until after I was kidnapped. My father was the type to walk around a bug."

"Times change."

"I suppose." Still, Skye knew that carrying a gun and being a dead shot wouldn't have prevented her abduction. Neither would any self-defense move she'd learned in the past nor would having a black belt in karate have prevented her being shot with a tranquilizer gun.

A sudden feeling of helplessness and panic rose out of nowhere, and she shuddered. Maybe it was a reminder not to try to move too fast. "Buttermilk, buttermilk," she whispered.

"Buttermilk? Sounds gross. Me, I'm ready for an iced cappuccino." Sally stood. "Looks like our poster girl is done with her workout. Let's hit the coffee shop."

WHEN BELLE DROPPED HER OFF, Skye was surprised to spot Sam sitting on her front porch drinking a glass of tea and talking to Gabe.

Both women got out. "What are you doing here, Sam?" Belle asked.

"Fine, thank you. And you?"

Belle punched her brother in the belly, then kissed his cheek. "Very well. I was just surprised to see you here."

"I was in the neighborhood, and I thought I might stop by for the lunch special at the Burrell-Walker buffet, but I forgot it was Thursday."

"You have to watch out for this one," Belle told Skye. "He's a freeloader, and his stomach is a bottomless pit."

"I'm used to Napoleon," Skye said, smiling. "Compared to him, Sam merely picks at his food."

Sam only grinned. "You ladies look cute. What have you been up to?"

"Cute? How patronizing. We've been at the dojo," Skye said, giving a yell and making one of the moves she'd just learned. "Don't mess with me. I might have to mop up the floor with you."

Sam roared with laughter. "You just might. I haven't practiced in a while."

Skye glanced from Sam to Belle. Belle shrugged. "All the Outlaws are pretty good. We started taking lessons when we were kids."

"Black belt, too?" Skye asked.

Sam nodded. "Say, how about I steal you away from Gabe

and Belle? We could drive to Austin and have lunch, then I could take you to your therapy session."

Skye glanced at Gabe. When he nodded, she said, "Sure. Sounds great. Let me go shower and change." She hesitated. "Will taking Gus into a restaurant there be a problem?"

"There's a place on South Congress that I know allows dogs on the patio if they're leashed. We can eat outside there. Okay?"

"I'll make it quick."

And she did. Skye was ready to go in just over twenty minutes. She put Gus's service vest on him, just in case there was a question, and grabbed a leash on her way out the door.

Sam waited alone on the porch. "What happened to Gabe and Belle?" Skye asked.

"Belle went home to change, and Gabe went along to help."

Skye stifled a laugh. "Wonder how long that will take?"

"I don't like to think about it. Say, what's with the thing Gus is wearing?"

"That's the vest that identifies him as a service dog."

"What kind of service are you talking about?"

"Gus is a trained service dog, an assistance dog. This vest gets him into all sorts of places. I usually don't put it on him when I go out since everybody around here knows him."

Sam frowned, still looking a little blank. "I don't get it."

"Have you heard of guide dogs for the blind?"

"Of course," he said as he opened the car door for them.

When they were on their way out of the compound, Skye said, "Guide dogs are service dogs. So are dogs trained to assist those with hearing problems or with other physical, mental or emotional disabilities. Gus is trained to help me."

"How?"

"By staying by my side, protecting me or alerting someone when I'm in distress. I sometimes have nightmares. When I do, Gus raises a racket on the intercom until Gabe or someone comes to wake me."

"I didn't know that. I just figured that Gus—well, I don't know what I figured. Who trained him?"

"I did, with the help of a professional consultant. I volunteered as a foster trainer during high school and college, so I knew quite a bit about the specialized training anyhow. We fostered several dogs, keeping each for a few months during their training program. Gus was originally Gabe's dog, the pick of the litter from breeding Kaiser to a friend's shepherd. I trained Kaiser as well, but he was getting along in years by then and wasn't as quick to learn as Gus."

"Gus takes his job seriously. I'll say that for him."

"Yes, he does. The trick is to refocus some of that training."

Sam grinned. "So that I can at least kiss you without his chewing off my pant leg."

"Yes." She smiled. "At least. How did you just *happen* to be in the neighborhood today?"

"I was on my way home from College Station, and I made a little jag in San Marcos."

Her heart began to pound. "What were you doing in College Station?"

"I went up yesterday to talk to people at Zelda's and do some checking around."

Her heart pounded faster. "And?"

"And I found out that a guy named Dennis Mayfield, who looks exactly like the sketch Flora made, worked delivering pizzas from Zelda's for a few months about the time you were abducted. The owner is checking through his back records to see if he can come up with any more information, like a social security number or the names of family members that might be on his application. It will take a couple of days. Two other members of the team are working some of the other universities where coeds went missing."

Skye leaned her head back against the seat. "I hope you find him."

"So do I, darlin'. So do I. I know you'll rest easier."

Would she rest easier?

Maybe. Even with the help of hypnosis, dealing with her long-standing emotional trauma was as difficult as redirecting Gus's deeply ingrained training.

"It couldn't hurt."

They made it to Austin and the restaurant on South Congress with the lunch crowd, and they opted to sit on the shaded patio with Gus. The Mexican place looked like little more than a shack from the outside, but it was a popular spot.

"Are you comfortable being here?" Sam asked. "You don't feel anxious, do you?"

"Not at all. I didn't even think about it."

"You've come a long way since I first met you."

She smiled. "I have, haven't I? A few weeks ago, I wouldn't have been here without an armed guard. If then. I'm glad we came here. I haven't been to Guero's in ages, and I know what I'm going to have. The black bean tamales. They're great. How about you?"

"Not sure yet, but it won't be black bean tamales. I haven't been here in a long time. Used to come a lot with one of my buddies. He kept hoping we'd run into Sandra Bullock."

"Did you?"

"Nope."

"Maybe she'll drop by today."

"I doubt it," Sam said, studying the menu. "I don't think she hangs out much in Austin anymore."

Sam ordered *queso flameado* and fish tacos. They debated about margaritas, then settled on iced tea instead.

She couldn't help but notice all the attention they got, especially from women who kept glancing their way. No way did she believe that Gus or the flaming *queso* delivered to their table generated all the stares and furtive peeks. Gus wasn't that much of a novelty, and she kept noticing the looks and nudges long after the fire died on the appetizer.

Women couldn't seem to keep their eyes off Sam. No

question that he was hugely hot; he certainly lit a major fire in her, but he seemed oblivious to the attention. Maybe he was used to it.

Or maybe it was because his focus was on her. Not that Sam missed much. Strike that. He didn't miss anything. Belle was like that, too. Probably from their law enforcement training. No doubt he could describe every person on the patio, but she was the center of his interest, and she could feel the intensity of their connection.

He wanted her. She could feel that, too. Even at high noon on a busy Austin street, with only their knees touching under the table, the air seemed to hum with sexual tension. She'd never felt desire so strong, so…palpable.

Why hadn't she left Gus at home? She wished that they could blow off lunch and her therapy session and check into a motel. She wanted to run her fingers through his hair and feel the faint stubble of his beard as he kissed every inch of her body. She wanted—

"Here you go. Black bean tamales for the lady, and fish tacos for the deputy."

Sam glanced up at the spike-haired server. "Thanks, kid."

"He's a Texas Ranger," Skye said, "not a deputy."

"Scu-u-use me. Need anything else?"

"More tea and more chips," Sam said, and the waiter hurried off. When he glanced back at Skye, he gave a slow grin that was surely designed to make women strip and throw themselves at his feet. "Saved by tamales and tacos."

"Pardon?"

"I was thinking seriously of skipping lunch, tying Gus to the table and checking into that motel down the street."

"Sam," she said in an admonishing tone. Then she laughed. "I was thinking the same thing."

"Don't tell me that, darlin'. I don't need much encouragement." He laid his hand over hers and his thumb slowly stroked her thumb.

"Eat your tacos, Sam."

"Yes, ma'am." He winked and dug in.

After lunch, they made it across town to Dr. Gossett's house just in time for her appointment.

The session went well, and Barbara was pleased with Skye's progress. "Want to cut the appointments back to one a week and see how it goes?"

Skye considered the suggestion, then agreed to forego the Sunday session. She felt terrific as she and Sam drove back to Wimberley—except for the strange desire to unbuckle her seat belt and crawl all over him as he drove.

Eager to get home, she considered and discarded a dozen ways for them to be alone, sans Gus. Unfortunately, she'd forgotten that her mother was having a committee meeting at the house, and a bunch of cars were parked out front.

"Looks like we're overrun with Mama's cronies," she said. "Want to run the gauntlet anyhow? If you can stay for dinner, I think there's chili in the freezer."

"Not this time, darlin'." He kissed her nose. "I need to get back to the office and write up a report before I call it a day. Are we on for this weekend?"

"Sure. Are we going dancing again Friday night?"

"If you want to. And when you're through at the office on Saturday, we'll skip out to somewhere that we can be alone. You game?"

"You betcha."

He kissed her.

She moaned.

Gus growled.

"Damn!"

Chapter Seventeen

Skye had spent every spare minute during the week on Gus's retraining. She'd brought a crate over from the clinic and put it in her sitting room. He'd learned easily to stay there quietly for longer and longer lengths of time while she went downstairs and left him alone.

Admitting the purpose behind the retraining made her feel a little devious and naughty, but necessary. She couldn't deny that she was eager to take her and Sam's relationship to the next level. She just hoped she didn't scare the poor man off—not that Sam was the type to scare easily. He acted as ready as she was. She hadn't been with a man since before her abduction, and it seemed as if all that suppressed libido was about to explode.

She also had to admit that her libidinous urges weren't the only thing drawing her to him. She adored Sam, all six-and-a-half feet of warm, fun-loving, sexy manhood. He made her feel strong and weak and reborn; she could hardly wait to see him again. Was that love? Had she ever really been in love? She'd thought she'd been in love with Jacob Merrill when they were in college, but that hadn't lasted, and her feelings for Sam were much…broader and more intense. What if this thing between Sam and her fizzled? The breakup with Jacob had been difficult; a breakup with Sam might be devastating. She didn't dare allow herself to dwell on the possibility that he was more interested in finding the kidnapper than he was in pursuing a long-term relationship with her. Thinking about it too much unnerved her.

Stop analyzing, Skye! Just enjoy the moment. Things will work out in due time—or maybe they won't. Don't be such a weenie.

Laughing at herself, she hurried upstairs to let Gus out of his crate and to take care of Nana and the puppies. The pups were thriving and darling little things. She was beginning to think that their sire was a champion digger instead of the fence jumper that Alice suspected.

What would she wear dancing at Fancy's tonight?

Something blue.

OF ALL THE DAMNED TIMES for Kim and her family to go out of town! Sam considered boarding Pookie in a kennel for the weekend, but he didn't have the heart. Nor did he want to take her with him to Wimberley. His plans didn't include Pookie. What was he going to do?

Sybil and Pat. Pat was a deputy sheriff in San Marcos. They had a little dog that they were crazy about. Max or Jax. Maybe he could talk them into dog-sitting for the weekend.

He called and sweet-talked Sybil into an invitation for Pookie. "You might like her so much, Sybil, that you might just want to keep her."

She laughed. "Forget it, you smooth-tongued devil. A weekend is my limit."

"I'm on my way."

Sam loaded Pookie in her carrier along with some of her other paraphernalia and broke a couple of speed limits on his way. He didn't want to be late to see Skye.

"Pookie, you're going to meet a new doggy friend. I'm sure you'll get along great."

Pookie and Jax, a Boston terrier, hated each other on sight.

They growled, barked, and Jax tried to bite Pookie, who ran to Sam and practically crawled his leg.

"I'm so sorry, Sam," Sybil said. "Jax is usually very friendly."

He forced a smile. "No problem. I appreciate the effort, anyhow."

Sam loaded Pookie and her stuff back into the pickup, cursed, then headed to Wimberley.

"Pookie, you can be a real pain in the ass."

She only yipped happily and settled in her carrier for a nap. He could manage for tonight, but tomorrow he was taking Skye and skipping town without the animals. Pookie could stay with Tiger and Gus. He hoped Skye was okay with the idea.

A few minutes later, Sam arrived at his destination and Gabe met him at the door. "We were about to give up on you, buddy."

"Dog problems," Sam said, lugging in Pookie and a sack of her stuff.

Pookie wiggled until Sam put him down, then she raced for Skye, who was coming downstairs.

She scooped him up. "Hello, sweetheart. Did you talk Sam into letting you come visit?"

"In a manner of speaking," Sam said drily.

"Go find Tiger," Skye said, setting Pookie on the floor.

Pookie took off like a streak toward the back of the house.

"Are we ready?" Gabe asked. "I'll let Belle know we're on the way."

Gabe went to get the car, while Sam and Skye waited on the front porch. "You look pretty tonight," Sam said, leaning down to kiss her.

"Thanks."

"Where's Gus?"

She smiled. "Upstairs."

His eyebrows went up. "Really?"

"Really."

"All right! Nervous without him?"

"Not yet. It's a first for me, but I figure that you, Gabe and Belle can handle anything that might come up."

"Count on it, darlin'."

SKYE DIDN'T MISS GUS AT ALL. She was too busy having fun. She danced and danced with Sam and Gabe and even once with Tim Olds. Thank heavens for yoga; she didn't get out of breath.

When they finally decided on one last slow dance before they called it a night, Sam pulled her close. "I can't believe that we're actually without animals tonight. And of all times to be double-dating. Think Gabe would drop us off at a motel on the way home?"

"Not likely," she said, chuckling. "He'd be indignant that you would even consider touching his baby sister. Anyhow, we mostly have bed and breakfasts, and all the owners know us. Remember, this is a small town. You know how that is."

"Don't I ever? My brother J.J. said half the people in Naconiche used to time his late-night visits with Mary Beth when they were dating."

"I'd love to meet your sisters-in-law sometime."

"They're all busy preparing for the stork right now. Maybe after the babies are born—" Sam's cell phone rang. And rang.

"Aren't you going to take that? It might be an emergency."

"That's what I'm afraid of." He took the phone from its case on his belt and glanced at the number. "Speak of the devil. It's J.J. Mind?"

"Of course not."

They went to the edge of the dance floor and Sam took the call.

"Well, congratulations, J.J. How's Mary Beth?" He listened for a while, then said, "I'm out boot scootin' with Skye, Gabe and Belle now. I'll tell her." He laughed at something his brother said. "Save it for me. We'll smoke it next time I see you. How's Carrie?" After a few minutes, he hung up. "J.J. and Mary Beth just had a boy. Seven pounds and thirteen ounces. Mother and baby are fine, but Katy is disappointed. She wanted a baby sister. Said she'd rather have a puppy. Frank's wife Carrie, is still hanging in there."

"That's wonderful news about the baby. What's his name?"

"You know, I didn't ask. Let me flag down Belle and tell her." He waved Belle and Gabe over and gave them the news.

"What did they name him?" Belle asked.

"I didn't ask."

"Men." Belle rolled her eyes at Skye. "Call J.J. back and find out."

Sam dutifully punched in the numbers of J.J.'s cell phone. "J.J., these women are driving me crazy to find out the baby's name. Call me back and let me know." Sam shrugged. "Phone's busy. He's probably calling everybody in the county."

The band broke into a swing, and the two couples said good night to the Olds and waved a general goodbye to other friends.

Skye notice that Gabe had a heavy foot on the way home, but she didn't comment. He and Belle were probably eager to be alone together as well.

"Sam, you interested in going fishing tomorrow?" Gabe asked as they turned off the highway.

"With you? No. Skye and I have other plans."

"You do? What?"

"Who made you tour director?"

Gabe laughed. "Belle, your brother's got a mouth on him."

"Tell me something I don't know."

Gabe pulled to a stop in front, and Skye said, "Are y'all coming in?"

"Not tonight," Gabe said. "Here's an extra key to the front door. Don't forget to reset the alarm. See you later."

Sam and Skye got out and watched while Gabe's car zoomed away.

"My brother certainly seemed glad to be rid of us."

"I know the feeling. Do we have to go in right now?"

Skye shook her head. "Want to do some stargazing?"

"Nope. I want to kiss you. Bad. And I don't want to worry about people and animals." He tossed his hat onto the hood of his pickup.

She tiptoed, and he bent to meet her mouth. His lips were hungry and she reveled in his urgency, meeting it with an urgency of her own.

"Oh, babe, I want you," he murmured. His teeth nipped the lobe of her ear as he cupped her bottom and pulled her against his hardness.

An aching like none she'd ever known unfurled deep inside, and they kissed again, his tongue plunging into her mouth.

The sound of a vehicle and the flash of car lights caused them to jump apart. This time it was Skye who cursed.

"What the hell!" Sam said.

"The patrol." She waved to the driver who was hidden behind the glare of the Jeep's headlights.

"Everything okay?" the driver called.

"Just fine, thanks." When the patrol left, Skye said, "I have an idea. Let's go over to the clinic. We'll have privacy there."

"Brilliant idea." He grabbed her hand and pulled her toward the pickup.

"Wait! Your hat."

He snatched up his hat, crammed it on his head and lifted her into the driver's side of the pickup. She scooted across while he fired up the engine and headed for the clinic. Once there, he pulled her from the seat and hot-footed it to the door.

"Uh-oh," she said. "I don't have my keys."

"I can break a window or jimmy the lock."

"The alarm's on, and it would bring the entire security force and Ralph."

He made a very succinct and profane response.

She echoed his sentiments.

"I have an idea," he said, grabbing her hand and installing her back in the pickup.

"Where are we going?"

"It's a surprise."

He drove out the gate and turned left, then left again.

"We're going to our picnic spot by the river?"

"Yeah. I don't figure anybody will be canoeing at this hour, do you?"

"Not likely."

They pulled to a stop in the grove by the river, and he killed the engine. A half moon glowed in a broken reflection as the river rippled over the sculpted limestone bed. Night insects and small frogs added their calls to the moving water sounds.

"Ever made out in a pickup before?"

"Not that I recall—or admit to."

He chuckled, reached across her, and her seat flew back into a full recline. Startled, she squealed.

"Oops," he said, "that wasn't a very cool move. Sorry about that."

"No problem. I just wasn't expecting it. The space is pretty cramped in here. Think we can manage?"

"We can manage. Darlin', I want you so bad right now, I could make love in a banana box."

The image struck her as funny, and she got the giggles. She tried to stop laughing, but she couldn't. He ignored her giggles and began to unbutton her shirt. When the last button was undone, he stripped it from her, then unsnapped her bra and tossed it somewhere behind him. He lowered his head, and his tongue touched her nipple. She gasped and sobered immediately.

"Like that?"

"I love that." She arched her back and moaned as he pulled

the nipple into his mouth. The sensation raced all over her body; she'd never felt anything so lovely.

A sudden loud thump on the hood almost stopped her heart. She raised her head and opened her eyes to peer over Sam's shoulder. Through the windshield, two glowing eyes stared back at her.

Skye screamed and bolted upright. Sam hit his head on the roof and cursed. "What the hell! Did I hurt you?"

A raccoon turned tail and scampered off the hood.

Feeling like a fool, Skye flopped back down, laughing and shaking her head. "No, you didn't hurt me, but a raccoon just about scared the pee-doodle out of me. He had his nose pressed against the glass, watching us. All I could see were two big black eyes."

"Maybe this wasn't such a good idea."

She pulled his shirt from his pants, unsnapped it with a *pop, pop, pop* and ran her hands over his chest. "It's a wonderful idea. Come here."

He didn't argue. He kissed her with a wildness that curled her toes in her boots. She began to fumble with the button and zipper of his jeans, and he was doing the same with hers.

His lips left her mouth and went back to her breasts. The sensation was incredible and almost overwhelming. "I hope you have protection," she gasped.

"I do." He stopped dead-still. "In my bag back at the house."

"Oh, no, Sam." She beat against his shoulders with her fists. "I may die."

He finished unzipping her jeans and skinned them down.

"Sam, we can't do this without protection."

"I'll keep my pants on, darlin'. This is for you."

He proceeded to do things to her that she'd never thought of in her wildest fantasy. He kissed her and murmured praises for her body and her movements and caressed her with an intimacy that drove her to an earth-shattering, cataclysmic orgasm. It sucked the breath from her with its power.

"Oh, Sam. I think I'm having a heart attack."

He chuckled and kissed her belly. "Did you like that?"

"I loved that. But what about you?" She reached to touch him.

He stopped her hand. "Don't, honey. I would blow like a roman candle."

She smiled. "I've always liked fireworks."

SKYE SHOULD HAVE KNOWN that she couldn't sneak in. Ralph was up waiting for them. She was sure she looked like she'd been doing exactly what she'd been doing. He didn't so much as raise an eyebrow. And if she wasn't mistaken, she thought she saw a twinkle in his eye. With Ralph, it was hard to tell.

"I'll lock up," Ralph said. "I've already taken Nana and Gus out for their evening constitutionals."

"Thanks, Ralph. Has Mama already gone to bed?"

He nodded. "Everybody has. It's well after midnight."

"Good night, Ralph," Sam said.

"Good night, Sam."

"Good night, Ralph," Skye said.

"Good night, Skye."

"Good night, John Boy," Sam said, and they all laughed.

Sam and Skye went upstairs and stopped in front of Sam's door. She glanced downstairs and noticed that Ralph seemed to be loitering around the alarm pad.

"I think he's hanging around to protect your honor," Sam said.

She giggled. "Too late." She tiptoed and kissed him on the cheek. "Good night."

"Can't you do better than that?"

"Not with Ralph watching."

She turned and hurried around the corner toward her room, and she heard Sam's door close behind her. She opened and closed her own door, staying in the hall and counting to fifty. She took off her boots, peeked around the corner to make sure the coast was clear downstairs and sneaked back to Sam's suite. Soundlessly, she opened the door to his sitting room and went inside.

Sam was in the bedroom, his boots and shirt off, unzipping his jeans.

She cleared her throat.

He looked up and smiled. "Need something?"

She nodded. "Did you say they were in your bag?"

He laughed and held out his arms.

Chapter Eighteen

Sam woke up feeling the best he'd ever felt in his life—and maybe the worst. Sky had been gone when he reached for her. She'd left sometime during the night.

Just as he'd first thought she had a shy personality, he'd figured she would be shy at lovemaking. Boy, was he wrong. She was something else. Playful and intense and energetic, she about wore him out. Not that he was complaining. It had been terrific, and he grew aroused just thinking about it—and anticipating more. That's why he felt so good.

Problem was, sometime during the night it had occurred to him that, while he wasn't looking, he'd fallen in love with her. Crazy, head-over-heels, make-a-fool-of-yourself in love. And that made him feel really bad. He hadn't planned on doing that. She was the same high-maintenance woman she'd been last week and the week before, and his net worth hadn't changed one iota, either.

Dumb, Outlaw. Dumb.

He ought to cut and run. Right now. But he could no more do that than he could rip out his heart. He didn't know how she felt about him; they hadn't discussed their feelings for each other, but he didn't think she was the kind of woman who would jump into bed without feeling something more than lust.

Was she?

Nah. He doubted that she'd been with a man in a long time. She hadn't been a virgin, but she'd been as tight as one.

How was he going to play this?

He took a shower and gave the question some more thought. He finally figured that he'd just let it ride. For the time being, anyhow. Sooner or later he'd have to face their problems, but there was no need borrowing trouble right now.

He quickly dressed and went downstairs. He was starving.

"WHAT ARE YOU AND SAM DOING this weekend?" Gabe asked Skye as he poured syrup on his pancakes.

"We're going fishing."

"Fishing? You?"

"Yes, me. We're going to his lake house this afternoon."

"That sounds delightful," Flora said. "The only bad thing about owning the Firefly Gallery now is that it cuts into my weekend frivolity. Sam, dear, I have a request."

Sam looked up from his plate. "Yes, ma'am?"

"While Skye is at the clinic this morning and Gabe is off showing land, why don't you come down to the gallery and let me sketch you?"

"I could do that. What time?"

"Any time after nine."

"Do I have to take my clothes off?"

Skye chuckled and Flora tittered. "What an idea!" Flora said. "I'll bet that would bring in business. But, no, I'm not planning a nude. Just wear a regular shirt and jeans. And your badge."

Gabe merely shook his head. "How about Belle and I join you at the lake?"

"You're not invited," Sam said, spearing another couple of pancakes from the platter.

Gabe raised his eyebrows.

Sam only grinned and chomped down on a sausage.

"Are you taking Gus?" Gabe asked Skye.

"To the lake? No. We're leaving the animals here. Ralph said he'd see after them. I talked to him before he and Suki left for San Marcos. They've gone over to the outlet stores. They should be back by noon."

Gabe looked as if he wanted to push the issue of taking Gus, but he didn't say anything, and Skye changed the subject.

The doorbell rang.

"That must be Napoleon," Skye said, rising. She put her hand on Sam's shoulder. "I'll see you at noon, and don't let my mother talk you into taking off your clothes." She laughed and fluttered her fingers.

Gabe walked her to the door, more out of habit than necessity. She didn't feel the need for an escort to her own front door any longer. Funny how much had changed so quickly.

"Skye—"

"Gabe, don't rain on my parade."

SKYE WOULD HAVE LOVED to cancel all her appointments and have slept in, but her conscience wouldn't let her, and she managed to make it through the morning without incident. She wasn't used to such an active night life—not that she was complaining. In fact, she was eager to leave for the fishing trip. She didn't care about the fishing; she was more interested in simply being with Sam.

He was sitting in the waiting room reading a magazine when she and Napoleon walked out with Mrs. Harold and Agnes, a calico with ear mites who was the last patient of the day.

Sam looked up from his magazine and winked at her. "Thought I might give you a lift." He stood and shook hands with Napoleon.

"Thanks. I need to pick up my bag at home. I'll be just a minute here."

"You go on, Dr. Skye," Napoleon said. "I'll see to things and lock up."

"Thanks. Have a good weekend. You, too, Judy," she said, waving to the receptionist.

When she and Sam were outside, he said, "Your bag is already in the pickup. Do you need to get anything else from home?"

"Lunch maybe. And I need to leave Gus with Ralph."

He motioned to the picnic hamper in the backseat. "Suki packed enough food for an army in that. Can you hold off for an hour or so until we get to the lake? We can get a Coke at a drive-in and snack along the way." He pointed to two bags on the dash. "You can have either banana chips or Cheetos."

"Sounds okay to me. Let's drop off Gus, and I'm good to go."

"Are you sure that you're okay with leaving him here?"

"Yes. He has more separation anxiety than I do, but we're working on it, and I think he'll do fine with Ralph."

At the house, Sam waited in the truck while Skye went inside, using her key and turning off the alarm. She knelt down to Gus, scratched his ruff and talked to him. He sat patiently, listening. After she was sure they had connected, she gave him a series of commands, and he trotted off to the back of the house. He passed Suki on his way. She carried a small insulated bag.

"You leaving?" Suki said.

"Yes, I just stopped to drop off Gus. Thanks for all the food."

"You're mighty welcome. Here's some cold bottled water and other drinks that might come in handy. You go on now. I'll reset the alarm behind you. Y'all have a good time. Don't worry about bringing home any fish."

Feeling almost giddy, Skye gave her a hug, then hurried out to the truck and climbed in. "Suki gave me drinks. Head 'em up! Move 'em out!"

Sam laughed and stepped on the gas.

She ate the banana chips before they got to Dripping Springs—in between feeding Sam Cheetos.

"You only wanted me to do this so you wouldn't get orange fingers."

"Smart girl."

"I haven't been a *girl* in a lo-o-ong time."

"Sorry, darlin'. Stick your fingers over here, woman, and I'll lick 'em clean."

"Thanks, but I've got another wipe in my bag." She started rummaging around with her left hand.

"If you're worried about germs, after last night, I think it's too late. We traded about everything."

Skye chuckled. "You're right about that. Here." She leaned over and held out her index finger.

He licked it several times, then took it into his mouth up to the second knuckle and sucked. A sharp sensation shot through her breasts, and she almost came out of her seat belt.

Pulling her finger away, she said, "I'd better find the wipe."

"Did I hurt you?"

"No, but I have another finger and a thumb to go, and we might have a wreck."

He glanced at her, frowning. "A wreck?"

"When I attack you."

He gave a bark of laughter. "Woman, you are something else."

"Is that bad?"

"No, darlin', you don't hear me bellyaching. It's good. Very good. I just figured that you'd be…well, sort of skittish. And maybe a little shy."

"I've never been shy. Phobic as hell, but not shy. I haven't been with a man in a long, long time, and I think you've unleashed a tiger in me. With you, I feel totally uninhibited. Is that a problem?"

He glanced over and grinned. "Not as long as you keep your seat belt buckled."

"If we're going to keep talking about this, you'd better turn up the air conditioner."

He twisted a knob.

She burst into laughter. "Sam, you're shameless."

"I won't deny it."

"Have you had any luck tracing Dennis Mayfield?"

"Are you changing the subject?"

"You noticed. Well, have you located him?"

"Not yet, but the team's working on it. We're circulating the sketches to the other university towns where girls were kidnapped."

"You know, I've never known much about the other cases. Did he collect a lot of money? If he did, it seems strange that he'd keep on abducting people."

"Does seem peculiar, doesn't it? But I don't think his motive was just the money. He got spooked at the pickup a couple of times and left without the cash. He managed to collect on three, but he didn't make good on his promise to turn over the victims. One of the girls was from a family who couldn't afford to pay, and you were found before Gabe had to make the drop."

"How much did he get away with?"

"Well over a million dollars."

"And he worked delivering pizzas in College Station?"

"As I said, I don't think that the money was his primary motivation. If it was, he could have invested his cash with A.G. Edwards and skipped to Mexico."

She shuddered. "Do you think you'll ever catch him?"

He patted her leg and left his hand on her thigh. "Don't ever doubt it. With the help you were able to give us, we'll find the bastard."

"I wonder if he stopped after me, or if he just moved his operations to another state."

"We're checking that possibility, too. Don't worry. His days are numbered. We're covering all the bases, including considering a story on *America's Most Wanted* if it comes to that. Would you be game?"

"I don't relish being on TV, but if it would help capture him, I'd do it. The families of all the people he murdered deserve that."

"Let's not talk about that scumbag anymore," Sam said. "Let's talk about sex instead." He winked and gave her a devilish grin.

"Let's not. Oh, I forgot to ask. Did J.J. call you back?"

"Yep. The kid's name is John. John Wesley Hardin Outlaw, the third. Isn't that a mouthful to stick on a baby? My grand-daddy would be tickled, and my daddy is about to bust his buttons over it."

"Do you want to name your children after famous outlaws?"

"Nah. Except there have been so many bad hombres around that you can't pick any good names that one of them hasn't had. Except maybe Percy or Durwood, and I wouldn't hang that on a kid."

"Nor would I. What if you had to go through life as Skye Walker? People ask all the time if my father was Native American."

"Why did they name you that?"

"Who knows? Their hippie roots I suppose. There are lots of people my age running around with names like River and Sunbeam. I suppose I should be happy that it isn't something worse."

"True. There was an outlaw named Big Nose Kate."

She made a face. "Think I'll stick with Skye."

The ride to the lake passed quickly, and Skye was surprised when Sam pulled up into the carport of a small stone house on a bluff and said, "Here we are."

"Oh, Sam, this is beautiful." It had a big yard, big enough for Gabe to land his helicopter, with a grove of trees in the rear. She got out and ran to the back. Steps, carved from the limestone, led down to the boat house below. "Is there a boat in there?"

"Yep."

He draped an arm over her shoulders. "And we'll go out later. Let's eat first. Those Cheetos are a distant memory."

After he unlocked the door and turned off the alarm, she carried the food inside, and Sam brought the rest of their stuff. They left the basket and cooler in the kitchen and opened the windows to air out the place.

The house was small with wood and tile floors and a stone fireplace, but it was nicely decorated with simple masculine furniture and had an incredible view she'd glimpsed as she opened the shutters.

"I really like your house. I'll bet it was hard to leave it and move to San Antonio."

"In some ways. I built it when I was first stationed in Austin. I won the land in a poker game years ago."

"In a poker game? It must have been a huge pot."

"Fair-sized. But the guy who put it up thought he had a winning hand for sure, and he'd been losing all night. He had more money than he had good sense."

"And he lost again."

Sam nodded. "Four deuces beats a full house any day of the week."

"I don't know much about poker."

"I'll teach you. Let's eat, and I'll show you around the house. I sure hope Suki sent some chili." He opened the basket and peeked in.

There was a bounty of choices, and after lunch, they moseyed down the back steps, and Sam got his bass boat out.

Skye slathered on sunscreen, plopped on a hat and climbed in. "I hope you know where you're going," she said as he pulled out of the cove and headed toward open water. "This is a big lake," she shouted over the roar of the engine as they bumped over the water.

"I know every in and out. I've spent a lot of time on the water, and I'm going to take you where the fish are."

"What kind of fish?"

"Bass, I hope. Say, I just remembered. Since you're a vegetarian, how do you feel about catching fish?"

"I feel okay about it. I even eat fish occasionally. But if it's all right with you, I'd rather release anything I catch. *If* I catch anything. Gabe's the fisherman in the family, not me. How do you know where the fish are?"

"This morning I called a buddy of mine who's a guide. He gave me a couple of leads."

A short time later, they stopped near a gallon plastic jug that acted as a buoy. "What's that?"

"A marker that Bill Pike put out. There should be some fish here." He picked up a rod with a simple-to-operate reel. "You know how to handle one of these?"

"I think so. What do I use for bait?"

"A purple worm."

"What kind of worms are purple?"

"Artificial ones. There's sort of like gummy worms, except that they're plastic." He opened his tackle box and attached the purple wiggly. "There you go." He gave her a quick refresher course in how to cast with the rod and reel. "Got it?"

"Got it." She rubbed the worm between her fingers for a moment, then executed a perfect cast.

"Good girl! Uh, sorry, *woman*. I thought you were a novice."

"I used to be pretty good. Remember, I grew up on a river. I just haven't fished in years." She felt a strike. "I've got one!"

"Already? Play him slow and easy, now." Sam watched as she brought the fish to the boat, then he grabbed the line and held up the large-mouthed bass. "Look at the size of this thing. Must be at least five pounds. You sure you want to release him?"

"I'm sure."

Sam gently removed the hook, lowered the fish into the water and let it go. He put a purple worm on his own line and cast into the area where she'd caught her fish. She cast again in another area and immediately got another strike.

They fished for an hour. She caught five bass, and he didn't even have a nibble. "What's your secret darlin'?"

"Clean living and a pure heart."

He laughed. "Besides that."

"Reel in your line." He did as she requested, and she captured the end of his line and held the worm for a moment, rubbing it in her fingers. "Now try it."

He cast in the same spot where he'd been fishing, but this time his line got hit almost immediately. "Hot dam, darlin'!! I've got a monster." He worked the fish and finally reeled in a huge specimen, the biggest one yet. "Look at that beauty! I'll bet it weighs seven or eight pounds. Lordamercy. Just get a load of that. That's dinner for four."

She chuckled, loving his excitement. "Are you going to keep it?"

"Bet your boots." He glanced up at her and lifted his eyebrows. She shrugged. "Aw, hell," he said, then let the fish go.

"Sam, don't feel you have to do that for me. I don't mind, honestly."

"No big deal. This way I don't have to clean them, and I'd rather have chili anyhow."

They fished for another hour. Skye stopped after she'd caught a couple more, and Sam grew bored getting one strike after another. He pulled in his line as well.

"I want to know what you did," he said.

"When?"

"You know when. What did you do to those purple worms?"

"I just rubbed them for luck."

He cocked an eyebrow and stared at her for a moment. "I don't know what it is about you, but I know it's something. Tell you what. I'll buy a bunch of worms, and you can rub them, and we'll sell them for fifty dollars a piece. Hell, a hundred dollars a piece. We'll make a killing." He grinned.

She knew he was teasing, but she shook her head, then leaned over and kissed him. "Luck doesn't last forever."

"Oh, I don't know about that. I've always been lucky. Luckiest day of my life was when I walked into that party and spotted you. Ready to go in?"

She nodded. "More than ready."

Chapter Nineteen

"I'm so glad this place is open again," Skye said as they sat on one of the decks overlooking the lake. "I have fond memories of it."

The Oasis was an old tradition in the Austin area, although lightning had sparked a devastating fire some time ago. Now rebuilt, the restaurant was on a cliff four or five hundred feet above the water, and a series of decks were built at various levels below. Tables with colorful umbrellas were filled with people drinking margaritas and enjoying the view. Sunsets were always spectacular.

They sat with a crowd of tourists and locals watching the sun shimmering its orange glow over the water and painting the horizon in golds, reds, pinks and blue.

"To sunsets," Sam said, touching his drink to hers.

"To sunsets."

They sipped and held hands as they watched the last vestige of the sun sink below the horizon. They, along with the other patrons, burst into applause at the finale of nature's show.

"Spectacular," she said, warmed from the beauty of the display.

She glanced at Sam, but he wasn't watching the sunset, he was watching her. "Spectacular." He squeezed her hand. "Let's have dinner and get home."

She smiled. "Let's eat fast."

SAM LIFTED SKYE from the pickup cab and swung her around. "I thought that waiter was never going to bring the check."

Laughing, she caught his shoulders as he let her slide down the length of his body. "He was slow, wasn't he? It must have taken him a minute and a half."

"That's a minute too long." He kissed her nose, then turned to unlock the door and disarm the alarm system. He flipped on the lights, then stood back to let her pass. She hesitated a couple of seconds.

"Old habits die hard," she said. "Sorry."

"Don't be sorry." He stepped inside, drew her after him and reset the alarm. "Want to stay here and let me check out the house?"

She nodded. "I thought I was over all my anxieties, but a little bit must have been hiding in a corner. And I feel a little naked without Gus and in a strange place. Do you mind?"

"Not at all. The kitchen's clear unless somebody is a contortionist and can fit in one of those cabinets or the oven. Want me to check?"

"I think you can skip the kitchen."

He heard him going from room to room, opening doors and calling, "Clear. Clear." In a couple of minutes, he was back. "Nobody under the beds or in a closet. I did find quite a bit of dust, though. Can you live with that?"

She smiled. "I can live with that."

Sam unclipped the gun from his belt and laid it on the mantle, unpinned his badge and left it there, too. "You're really missing Gus?"

"A little. I'm used to having him by my side all the time." She walked to where he stood by the fireplace and put her hands on his chest. "But you're a pretty good substitute."

"Gee, thanks." He rubbed his nose against hers.

"Your nose isn't as cold, and you kiss lots better." She fingered a snap on his shirt. "I like that you wear western shirts."

"You do? Why?"

"'Cause they open so easily." She pulled out his shirttail, popped open the front and ran her fingers through the soft hair on his chest. "I love the way that feels. So soft." She rubbed her cheek against the downy mat and smiled when she felt him tense.

"We're going to have to get you some western shirts," he said, reaching for her buttons and fumbling with them. "Oh, hell," he said finally and ripped her blouse open, sending button missiles flying. "I'll sew them back on later," he said, then kissed her neck as he tossed aside her blouse and unhooked her bra.

"You can sew?"

"A button? Yes, ma'am." He pulled her close, working her breasts over his bare chest. "Boy, that feels good."

He put his hands under her bottom and lifted her up so that he could reach her breasts with his mouth. She wrapped her legs around his waist, arched her back and offered him what he wanted.

His mouth and his tongue did glorious things, and she sucked in a huge gasp. "Oh, Sam."

"Yes, ma'am?"

"Do that some more."

"I intend to. I love these." He held her with one arm and moved the other hand over each breast, weighing, stroking, cupping to take a tip into his mouth and suck.

She moaned, and he strode toward the bedroom, still holding her, her legs still around him. He laid her gently on the bed, and his eyes never left her as he stripped off his boots and jeans.

"You are so beautiful," she said.

"That's my line, darlin'. And you're beyond beautiful. I wish I could think of enough words to say how amazing you are." He pulled off her sandals and her shorts, tossing them over his shoulder.

"You're doing very well."

"Lordamighty, I hope so. The minute I touch you, my brain turns to mush." His hands stroked the length of her leg as he crawled in bed beside her, first outside the outside curve, then inside. "You're skin is so soft." He ran his tongue along the inside of her thigh. "And tastes so good."

He nipped and nibbled and explored as she drowned in mind-blowing sensation. Nothing had ever prepared her for this. Surely she would die if he didn't end it soon.

But she didn't want it to end.

"I want you," she whispered, reaching for him.

He rolled away. "Not yet." He stripped away her panties at a maddeningly slow pace, following their trail with his tongue, then kissing the bottom of each foot before he returned.

He looked into her eyes, stroked her cheek with his fingertips and outlined her lips. "I love you so much," he whispered. He ran his hand down her neck and cupped her breast and murmured the same words against her ear.

She stilled. What had he said? Had she misunderstood? His breathing was as ragged as hers. All she could respond was, "Oh, Sam. Tell me again."

"I love you."

She couldn't help herself. She went absolutely wild with urgent desire. His briefs went flying, and she rolled until he was on his back with her straddling him. She was just about to guide him inside when he yelled, "Wait!" and reached for the drawer of the night stand.

He was too slow. She grabbed the condom, rolled it on him and impaled herself on his hardness.

She moved once, twice, then went through the roof and shot to the stars as she spasmed with sensation that seemed to go on and on and on. He stiffened and began to throb inside her. She reveled in the feelings until she felt him relax.

Collapsing on top of him, she laid her cheek on his chest. "Oh, Sam. I think I love you, too."

"Think?" He stroked her back with slow movements.

She signed. "No, I'm sure. Do you mind?"

She felt the rumble of his chuckle against her cheek. "Why would I mind?"

She propped up and looked at him. "Because I'm such a mess. And—and I'm a *vegetarian*."

He barked a laugh. "Is it catching?"

Skye joined in his laughter. "Just don't expect me to cook you a steak or a meat loaf."

"Honey, I don't even like meat loaf very much. And I can cook my own steak. Are you going to force-feed me tofu and sprouts?"

"No. I don't even know why I said that. I suppose it just il-lustrates how very different we are."

"And how are we so different?"

"A dozen ways. You're a realist, and I'm…not. You're brave and gutsy, and I struggle with years of fear. I'm a wimp. I'll bet a hundred dollars our politics are polar opposites. Who did you vote for in the last presidential election?"

He told her.

"There! I knew it. Didn't I tell you? I think that guy is a dork. What are we going to do?"

"How about we go have dessert?"

"Dessert?"

"Yep. I've worked up an appetite, and you were so hot to trot that you wouldn't let me take time to get any pie at the restau-rant."

"Hot to trot? *Me?*" She grabbed a pillow and whacked him. "*Me?* You're the one who took my fork away and wiped my mouth." She whacked him again.

Sam covered his head. "Don't darlin'. I'm too worn out to defend myself."

NOW HE'D SCREWED THE POOCH, Sam thought as he lay in bed with Skye cuddled next to him, sound asleep. He hadn't meant to tell her that he loved her, but now there was no going back. They'd talked a lot but not about the implications of what loving each other meant. Not about the future. Not about a long-term relationship. Not about marriage.

Oh, he knew it was too soon to be thinking about marriage, but at their ages, it was a logical step somewhere down the line. And sticking his head in the sand wasn't going to make their problems go away. He didn't give a damn about her politics—his mother and dad voted for different people half the time. That was no big deal. He felt the same way about their differences in religion; he didn't see a dime's worth of different between dunkin' and sprinklin' if your heart was in the right place. Those were minor problems as far as he was concerned. He was bothered by other things.

She'd surprised him about the motorcycle. And she didn't seem to be bothered by the dangers inherent in being a Ranger—at least she hadn't mentioned it. But, as he saw it, his job was a major obstacle. As glamorous as everybody considered the Texas Rangers, the pay sucked. With his years of experience, a sergeant in the Austin Police Department made a lot more than he did as a sergeant in the Texas Rangers—and that wasn't enough to provide the things Skye was used to.

But it was who he was. He'd never wanted to be anything but a Texas Ranger. He loved it, and he sure wasn't willing to give it up to sell real estate or peddle life insurance. He'd be climbing the walls within a week. Hell, within a day.

Skye was a lot better about things than she'd been when they first met. She didn't need a corps of bodyguards walking in lock-step around her any longer, and she seemed pretty secure just to have him around. Him and Gus. But what would happen if he had to go out of town for a couple of days? He often did because of the nature of his job with the unit. Could she handle it? He didn't think so. That was just one of a dozen problems a hell of a lot more serious than whether or not she ate barbecued ribs.

His townhouse was fine for him, but what would happen if he added another person and a big dog? And what about her practice? If they got together, even for a trial run, somebody would have to commute. And that wasn't practical. He got a headache thinking about all the complications, and acid rose in his throat.

He shouldn't have had that second piece of pie.

THE NEXT MORNING, while Sam made coffee, Skye scrambled the half-dozen eggs that Suki had sent along and popped some freezer waffles in the toaster.

When Sam dug in, he said, "I thought you told me you couldn't cook."

"This is about the extent of my skills. How about you?"

"I'm a terror with a George Foreman Grill."

"I can make a pretty good grilled cheese sandwich, and I can put together a salad and peel an orange."

"Sounds like between us we could cover the basic food groups," Sam said.

"Except for chocolate. What's your favorite candy bar?"

"Snickers."

"Me, too! I love those things. Of course, I love anything chocolate."

The rest of the day they talked and ate and made love, then started the sequence all over again. They never did drop a hook in the water.

Toward evening, they packed the car and cleaned up the house, both hesitant to leave.

"I love it here," Skye said. "It's so peaceful and lovely."

"We'll come back often."

"Promise?"

"I promise. Ready?"

"As ready as I'll ever be."

Skye stepped outside the door while Sam set the alarm and locked up. A big red tabby came up to her and rubbed against her legs. "Well, hello, big guy. Where did you come from?" She squatted down to stroke his head.

He sat quietly, blinking lazily and purring.

The minute Sam started toward them, the cat shot from the carport and ran into the brush. "Well, I'll be damned," Sam said.

"About what?"

"That's Butch. He's a wild cat that hangs around the area and won't let anyone come near him. How'd you do that?"

She shrugged. "As I told you, I've always had a way with animals."

"You told me that you're weren't a Dr. Dolittle, either, but I'm beginning to think you are. You draw animals like a magnet. Even fish."

Skye hesitated to say more. She'd always been very private about that part of her life, sharing her gift with only a chosen few. Jacob, her former boyfriend had simply called her weird. That had hurt.

"I don't really understand the process myself, but animals and I seem to connect somehow. They don't talk to me for sure, but we connect. I can't explain it better than that. I think they recognize that they can trust me. Does it bother you? Do you think I'm weird?"

He smiled and gathered her into his arms. "It doesn't bother me, and I wouldn't call you weird, but I'd be lying if I didn't say that it's mighty peculiar. I thinks it's a handy talent to have if you're a vet. Have you always been able to do whatever it is that you do?"

"As far back as I can remember. My mother always said I was a fairy child."

She could feel the rumble of his deep chuckle. "Did she find you under a cabbage leaf?"

Skye laughed. "With my mother anything's possible. By the way, you never told me about your posing for her. How did she sketch you?"

"I don't know. She wouldn't let me see what she drew. Said I had to wait until the painting was done. I did keep my clothes on."

"Are you bragging or complaining?"

"I take the fifth."

Skye's cell phone rang, and Sam stepped away to let her answer it.

"Oh, hi, Mom." She listened for a moment, then said, "Hang on, I'll ask. Sam, my mother wants to know what time we'll be home and if they should set places for us at the table. Suki's making fried chicken."

"Tell her we're on our way."

"Mom, you said the magic words. We were just about to leave. See you in a little while."

As they backed out of the drive, Skye gazed longingly at the small stone house. She would always love this place. It was a little piece of heaven. As they drove away, she spotted Butch, sitting by a tree, flicking his tail and watching them go.

Chapter Twenty

The next two weeks seem to fly by in a blur of activity. Skye and Sam spent weekends together, one in Wimberley and one in San Antonio. She'd meant to call Lisa, her former roommate, when she was in San Antonio and get together with her, but it didn't work out. She and Sam were too busy with each other.

Lord, she was crazy about that man. She liked his cozy little townhouse and the neighborhood it was in. And she'd always loved San Antonio. They ate at a restaurant along the River-walk, and he bought her a balloon, a blue one.

"Blue's your favorite color, isn't it?" he'd asked.

"Actually, it's yellow. Yours is blue."

He went back and bought her a yellow one.

They went riding on his motorcycle and stopped for lime Snow-Kones and went home to make love with green tongues. Every day she fell more and more in love with Sam, and she began to think about long-term commitments. He hadn't brought up the subject, and she didn't want to, either, but she thought about it. She couldn't imagine anyone that she'd rather spend the rest of her life with, but marriage was a big step, and she didn't know if she was ready to face all the complications.

Oh, she felt safer now. She'd even begun to drive to Thursday morning karate lessons, but she hadn't tried to range further. The idea of driving to Austin or San Antonio by herself still caused her to break out in a sweat. And she couldn't imagine staying alone in the house at night, even with Gus and an alarm system.

"Be patient with yourself, Skye," Barbara Gossett had told her. "You're doing extremely well. Sam has been very good for you."

"He's a very special man."

Even Napoleon had commented on the changes in her. "You're sure happier these days, Dr. Skye. That Sam's doing?"

"Sam's and Dr. Gossett's."

"Have the Rangers found that man yet?"

An icy finger of apprehension touched her, and she shivered. "Not yet, but Sam says it's just a matter of time. They have some good leads."

That night when Sam called, as he did almost every night that they weren't together, she asked him about Dennis Mayfield.

"Nothing yet, but we're getting more and more information every day. We got a lead on what may be his sister. I'm going to Tyler tomorrow to check it out. Say, I've got some more news. Carrie, Frank's wife, just had a little girl this afternoon. They named her Lily."

"Oh, how wonderful. I know they're all excited."

"Yep. Sounded like it. I'm thinking about going to Naconiche this weekend and seeing the new babies and the family. Want to go?"

"Sure, I'd love to. Let me see if I can shuffle some appointments, and we can leave earlier on Saturday morning."

"That would be great. Did I mention that Mary Beth owns a motel? I'll bet I can get us a room at the Twilight Inn."

"Won't your parents be scandalized?"

"They're pretty open-minded, but if it would make you feel better, I can get two rooms, and we can sneak into one when the coast is clear. I'll make the reservation."

ON THURSDAY AFTER KARATE CLASS, Skye, Belle and Sally were gathered at the coffee house for their usual caffeine fix.

"Belle, I hear that you're a new aunt again," Skye said.

"Yes, a little girl. Carrie and Frank are thrilled, and their daughter Janey is over the moon to have a baby sister. Her twin brother Jimmy was pulling for a brother. Maybe next time."

"Is Lily an outlaw name?"

"I think it's a variation on Jersey Lilly, the saloon where Judge Roy Bean held court and hanged all the outlaws. Bean had a big crush on an actress named Lillie Langtry and named his place after her. Besides, I think Carrie liked the name."

"Works for me," Skye said.

"I hear that you and Sam are going to Naconiche this weekend," Belle said to Skye. "So are Gabe and I. We're having a family get-together to celebrate the new babies. Want to ride up together?"

"Okay by me, but you need to check with Sam."

"And another thing. I understand that Sam booked the last two rooms at the Twilight Inn for y'all, and we were hoping to stay there. There are two beds in every room. Mind if I bunk in with you? Gabe can stay with Sam."

Taken aback by Belle's suggestion, Skye was quiet for a moment.

Sally giggled. "That will certainly put the quietus on any hanky-panky."

Skye actually felt herself blush.

Belle laughed. "Sam and I can switch rooms when nobody's looking if you want."

"You'd better talk to Sam," Skye said. "This is his deal."

"I'll convince him," Belle said. "I'd sooner not stay with any of the family. Logistics problems. We'll work it out."

Skye finished her latte and said goodbye to her friends so that she could go home and get ready for a quick lunch, then her appointment with her therapist. And she needed to buy baby gifts after that.

Sam was probably going to hit the roof when Belle told him her plans. She was glad that was Belle's problem to deal with.

'NOT NO, BUT HELL NO," Sam told his sister. No way was he playing musical beds with Gabe and Belle. In the first place he didn't want to take any of those what-are-you-doing-to-my-baby-sister? looks from Gabe. And in the second place, he'd gotten to the rooms first. It was their tough luck.

But Belle had sweet-talked him the way she'd always been able to do every male in the Outlaw family, and, against his better judgment, he agreed to her horning in on his plans. Actually, he didn't tell her that their coming might be a good thing. It would save him some driving. Instead of going back to Wimberley to pick up Skye, he could drive over to Naco-niche from Tyler, a short hop compared to the five-hour trip to Wimberley, and spend Friday night with his folks. Skye could ride up with Belle and Gabe on Saturday morning.

He was in a bad mood when he hung up with Belle, not because of her call, but because the trip to Tyler might turn out to be a wild goose chase. The woman who was supposed to be Mayfield's sister had moved six months before, and he was going to have to spend extra time there trying to track her down.

Sam called Kim, his young neighbor, to see if she could look after Pookie for the weekend. She could. He'd call Skye that night to finalize plans with her, but he didn't anticipate any problems. She was cool about stuff like that; she wasn't the prima donna type.

SKYE CHANGED HER MIND A half-dozen times about what to wear and what to take. Belle had told her that things would be super casual, but still she wanted to make a good impres-sion on Sam's family. Oh, she'd met most of them at Belle's party, but things were different now. She and Sam were…were what? Dating? It seemed more than that.

She finally decided on an outfit, then packed her over-nighter and went down to breakfast. Gabe was already there, just finishing up.

He looked up from the paper. "Are you taking Gus?"

"Nope. He's staying with Ralph and Suki. I'll be fine without him."

And she *would* be, she emphasized to herself. Just fine. Her therapy sessions were helping her to become more and more confident. But she was glad that things had worked out so that Gabe and Belle would be along. This was the first time she'd ventured out into a strange place with a crowd—and so far from home. She doubted that the Twilight Inn had a security system.

A little flutter popped up in her stomach, but she tamped it down with a couple of "buttermilks." Amazing how that worked.

After breakfast, she and Gabe picked up Belle and were on their way to East Texas. The limestone hills with their small oaks and bushy cedar soon gave way to flatter land and farming country, then, still later, pine trees began to mix with the oaks. The pines grew taller and thicker as they approached timber country and the fertile rolling hills of the area. They made a pit stop for gas and to stretch their legs, and Gabe said they'd made excellent time.

A little before one, they crossed a bridge on a highway cut through a dense forested area of pines and mixed wood.

Belle pointed to a sign. "Naconiche City Limits. We're almost there."

"Thank God," Gabe said. "Next time we'll fly in the chopper. Is there a landing pad anywhere around?"

"I don't know," Belle said. "It's never come up, but I guess we could land in one of Frank's or J.J.'s pastures."

"But then, you wouldn't have a car to get around in," Skye said.

Belle directed the turns that took them around the court-house square of the small town. "There's the Double Dip," she said, pointing to her mother's ice cream shop. "Want to stop by and say hello before we check in? We can have a banana split for lunch."

"Maybe you can," Gabe said, "but I need something more substantial. And soon."

"The City Grill is right across the street," Belle told him. "They're safe for something simple. The Twilight Tearoom isn't open on weekends."

"Let me call Sam," Skye said. "I told him I'd phone when we got to town."

He answered on the first ring. "'Bout time," Sam said. "I was ready to give you up. Where are you?"

"Parked in front of the Double Dip and contemplating lunch. Belle says the tearoom isn't open on weekends."

"It is today," Sam said. "Come on out. We're waiting for you."

"We'll be right there." Skye relayed the message, and they drove to the tearoom.

Sam had told Skye the story of how Mary Beth, now J.J.'s wife, had come to town to claim an inheritance and found only a leaky Mexican restaurant and a dilapidated motel that was uninhabitable. Mary Beth, divorced and down to her last few dollars, and her daughter Katy had lived in the restaurant until she and friends could fix it up and turn it into a tearoom. Now it had a wonderful new roof, a pretty paint job and pots of red geraniums flanking the front door.

"Oh, an herb garden," Skye said as she got out of the backseat. She plucked a bit of rosemary and held it to her nose.

The door opened, and Sam stood there grinning. "Come on in."

"Hi, Aunt Belle!"

"Hi, Aunt Belle!"

"Hi, Aunt Belle!"

Three kiddos came charging to hug Belle's knees, and Skye smiled at them.

"Hey, munchkins," Belle said. "Let me introduce you to some special people. Dr. Skye and Mr. Gabe, these tornados are my nieces and nephew. Katy and Janey and Jimmy."

"Are you a doctor like Aunt Dr. Kelly?" Janey asked.

"No, I heard that she's a people doctor," Skye said. "I'm an animal doctor. A veterinarian."

A lovely tall redhead joined them. "I'm Kelly, Cole's wife, and I'm the people doctor." She shook hands with Gabe and Skye, then hugged Belle.

"And I'm Mary Beth, J.J.'s wife." The pretty blonde had a baby sling across her chest. "And this little sleeping fellow is John." She held open the sling for Skye and Belle to peek. "Welcome to the Twilight Tearoom. My helpers are setting up a buffet to hold us until the barbecue tonight. Carrie and Lily aren't here for obvious reasons, but the party this evening is at their house."

"When she's just had a baby?" Skye asked, incredulous.

Mary Beth laughed. "Carrie will be directing from the chaise. Frank and the housekeeper have everything under control. I offered to have the party at our house, but she wouldn't hear of it. We're all bringing something and the guys are going to cook outside. Ah, here comes the food. We have potato and leek soup, chicken tortilla soup, spinach quesadillas and a variety of salads, sandwiches and fruit."

"Oh, my," Skye said. "This looks wonderful."

Belle hugged Mary Beth. "I don't know how you do it."

"I have a great staff," Mary Beth said.

"Don't let her kid you," Sam said. "Mary Beth is an awesome cook. Look at the success of this place. It's packed every day at lunch."

Belle hugged Cole and J.J., and Skye and Gabe greeted the brothers as well.

"And who is this little one?" Skye asked Cole, who held an adorable baby with red curls.

"This is Elizabeth."

Elizabeth flashed a wet smile, showing small teeth amid the drool. She held out her arms to Skye, and Skye couldn't resist the dimpled baby. She took the child into her arms.

"Hello, pretty baby."

Elizabeth laughed and patted Skye's cheeks. "Pee!"

Skye looked at Cole. "Is she telling me something?"

He grinned. "I think she's returning the compliment. She's trying very hard to talk. Let me take her off your hands so that you can get a plate."

Elizabeth was having none of it. She clung to Skye like a monkey.

"She's okay," Skye told him.

"I'll get your plate," Sam said. "Want to come along and tell me which of this stuff you can eat?"

"Do you have dietary concerns?" asked Mary Beth.

"I'm a vegetarian."

"No problem. Let me serve you. Do you eat eggs and dairy?"

"Yes."

"Sam," Mary Beth said, "get her some soup, and I'll do the rest."

"I can handle it," Skye said, parking Elizabeth on her hip. "You don't need to be waiting on me. You have a new baby yourself. Just tell me what's what."

"Any of the salads are okay except the one with ham at the back. The chips are fried sweet potato. Those sandwiches are roast beef, those are turkey and those are egg salad."

"And these are Elvis sandwiches," said little Katy, who was filling her plate. "He was the king."

"Elvis sandwiches?" Skye asked.

"Grilled peanut butter and banana," Mary Beth told her. "The kids love them."

"Not just the kids," J.J. said, snagging a quarter. "I love these things. Try one."

She added one to her plate and carried it to the table where Sam had put their soup, hers potato-leek, his tortilla. Kelly joined her and tried to take Elizabeth, but she refused to budge. And she wouldn't sit in the high chair that Cole brought.

"Don't worry about it," Skye said. "I'm used to wiggly little creatures."

She planted the baby on her thigh, handed her a cracker and tasted the raspberry tea with one hand while she anchored Elizabeth with the other.

Sam and Cole joined them, while the children sat in a red booth and the rest of the adults at the next table.

They talked and laughed and ate. The food was wonderful, and Skye adored the Elvis sandwiches.

"Where are your parents?" Skye asked Sam.

"Mom's running the store, and Dad's out helping Frank get set up for tonight. They'll both be at the shindig later."

"Looks like we need to get home and put Elizabeth down for her nap," Kelly said. "Her eyes are drooping." She stood and plucked the baby from Skye's lap without a fuss. "Skye, you're a sweetheart for holding her."

"I enjoyed it."

Elizabeth tucked her head on her mommy's shoulder and closed her eyes. Cole stood and grabbed the diaper bag hanging from the back of his chair. "See y'all later. We enjoyed talking with you, Skye."

"What about me?" Sam asked.

"What about you, squirt?"

Sam grinned at his oldest brother and unfolded his six-and-a-half-feet length. "I stopped being squirt when I grew tall enough to look you square in the eye." He clamped Cole on the shoulder and kissed Kelly's cheek. "See you later."

Skye loved the easy comradery and teasing of all the Outlaws, and she liked Mary Beth and Kelly very much. And the whole family seemed to have taken Gabe and her into their fold quite naturally. The Outlaws were a really nice family— and talk about feeling safe. How could she not?

After Cole and Kelly left, J.J. stood. "Folks, I've got to ice down a half-dozen watermelons, and Mary Beth looks a little tuckered out to me, so I'm going to take my bunch and the twins home to rest before the party. I imagine there are some old guys over at the office anxious to check you into your rooms. We'll see you out at Frank and Carrie's place about five or so. Need anything before we leave?"

Belle raised her eyebrows and glanced at the others. When no one spoke up, she said, "I think we're fine, J.J. Mary Beth, thanks for the fantastic lunch."

Skye, Gabe and Sam echoed the thanks. "And, Mary Beth, you'll have to give me the recipe for the Elvis sandwiches," Skye said. "They're fabulous."

Mary Beth chuckled. "No recipe to it. Spread some peanut butter on a piece of bread, lay banana slices on that, slap another piece of bread on that, butter the outsides and grill until it's golden brown. I started making them one day out of desperation and an empty cupboard."

"Well, they're terrific, and I think that even I could make them."

They all walked out together, said their goodbyes and moved Gabe's car over to the motel parking lot. The car was blazing hot from sitting in the sun, and Skye was sweating from the humidity by the time they drove the short distance.

An octogenarian who looked as if a gust of wind would knock him over came hurrying out of the office. Another old man hurried after him.

"I'm B.D.," the first one said. "And this here is Howard. You don't have to worry about registering. Sam took care of that. Hiddy, Belle. Good to see you home. You ladies are in three, and the gents are in four. Howard's got the keys."

Howard handed out keys with plastic tags to everybody. "We'll tote your bags inside if you'll open the trunk."

"We can get them," Gabe said, popping the trunk with his remote.

"No sir-ee bob," B.D. said. "That's part of the service, and it keeps us fit. Which ones belong to which?"

Gabe pointed out the women's bags, and B.D. grabbed one in each hand and took off to unit three. Howard took the other and headed for unit four in the strip of rooms separated by a carport between each.

Belle unlocked their door and held it open for B.D., who bustled inside the gloriously air-conditioned room and placed a bag on each luggage rack at the foot of the beds.

The unit with its soft peach walls and muted peach and green-and-yellow plaid spreads and curtains was quite attractive, and a green stuffed chair in the corner looked inviting. The place even smelled faintly of peaches, and a small bouquet of yellow daisy mums sat on the nightstand between the beds.

"I think you'll find the place real comfortable," B.D. said. "Bathroom's through that door yonder, and over there is what we call the kitchenette. The icebox is stocked with drinks and doodads for snacks, and there's a coffee pot and fixins on the counter by the microwave. And here's a bowl of fruit. There's some more stuff in the cabinets, little boxes of cereal and such if you're amind to have yourself some breakfast in the morning. We also got us a new ice machine down at the office if you want some extra."

"Thanks, B.D.," Belle said, handing him a couple of dollars.

He pocketed it quickly and nodded. "There's maps and such by the telephone, but I don't 'spect you'll be needing them, Belle." He cackled at his little joke.

"No, I think I can find my way around."

"Your mama said to give her a call when you got settled in."

B.D. left, and no sooner had the door closed when the phone rang.

Skye turned the dead bolt and put on the safety chain while Belle answered the phone. "Hello, Gabe. Long time, no see." She winked at Skye while she listened. "Just a minute. Skye, do you want to take a grand tour of the town and stop by the Double Dip? That should take about ten or fifteen minutes."

"Sure. I'd love to see the famous Double Dip and say hello to your mother."

A few minutes later, they gathered outside at Gabe's car and took the guided tour, mostly around the court house square where Belle pointed out Carrie's office as well as the sheriff's department, the City Grill, the drugstore and the feed store that doubled as a bus stop. They drove a short distance to pass by the library and the hospital.

"Kelly's office is in that building," Belle said pointing to a place across the street from the hospital, "and she and Cole live two blocks away. Turn left here, Gabe."

They drove by Kelly and Cole's house, a pretty cottage with a garage apartment in back, then went back downtown to end up at the Double Dip.

When they went inside the shop with its lovely cold-sweet scent of peppermint and strawberry and chocolate, Nonie Outlaw met them at the door, arms wide. She hugged everybody. "Didn't I see you stop by earlier?"

"We were going to come in and have a banana split for lunch," Belle said, "but Gabe insisted on real food."

"I saved room for dessert," Gabe said. "I hear you make the best in the business."

"Well, sit down at the counter, young man, and I'll make one for you. What will the rest of you have?"

Everybody else passed.

"I'm sorry that I couldn't have lunch with all of you," Nonie said as she split a banana, "but Wes is out helping Frank, and I swear everybody in the county came to town today and ended up at the Double Dip. And of all days, my usual helper is sick with a terrible summer cold."

"Can we do anything to help?" Skye asked as she took a seat on a red counter stool.

"Do you know anything about ice-cream parlors?" she asked as she worked on the concoction for Gabe.

"I've frequented plenty, and I worked in one in Wimberley one summer when I was in high school. That was a long time ago, but I think I can still fix a soda. What do you need?"

"I didn't know that," Sam said.

"I'm a woman of mystery," she returned with a haughty air.

Nonie smiled. "I need somebody to relieve me for a few minutes while I run upstairs and finish the squash casserole and the green beans for tonight."

"No fudge pie?" Belle asked.

"The fudge pie is already made."

Skye went around the counter, put on an apron and washed her hands. "Show me where things are."

Nonie pointed out the various ingredients and implements. "I'll be as quick as I can."

"Take your time."

Nonie hurried away, and Sam cleared his throat. "I've changed my mind. I think I'll have a…uh…a root beer float."

"Coming right up." Skye grabbed a frosty mug from the freezer, filled it half full of root beer from the fountain, added two scoops of vanilla ice cream, then topped it off with a bit more root beer to make it foam. She popped in a straw and set it on a napkin in front of him. "That will be five dollars."

"*Five* dollars?"

"Yep," Skye said. "The extra charge is for thinking I couldn't do it and would end up with a foamy mess." She laid a spoon beside his mug and held out her hand.

Belle whooped with laughter and poked her brother. "She gotcha. Pay up, buddy."

Sam grumbled, but he finally pulled a bill from his wallet and slapped it in Skye's hand.

She only had to make a small chocolate sundae and a double dip strawberry cone with chocolate sprinkles before Nonie came back downstairs.

"All done," Nonie said. "I'll just have to pop them into the oven when we get there this evening." She hugged Skye. "Thank you, dear."

"You're welcome." Skye smiled, feeling prouder of herself than she had in ages.

Chapter Twenty-One

Who could believe it? Skye thought as she accepted a glass of wine from Frank. She felt so normal here. And she hadn't said "buttermilk" once since she'd been in Naconiche.

"Anybody else need anything?" Frank asked. "Carrie, are you okay?"

"I'm fine," Carrie said, "Now shoo, love. Go cook something on the grill. I'm starving."

After Frank left, Skye said, "I can't believe you're hosting a party when you had a baby three days ago."

"I'm only playing lady of the manor, which I do very well," Carrie said from her spot in an easy chair. "Lift that barge! Tote that bale!"

Mary Beth laughed. "I think you have that backward."

"Whatever," Carrie said with a flutter of her fingers. "Actually, it's much easier for me to be here. I can go to bed if I get tuckered out—which I don't see happening when Frank won't let me move. And to tell the truth, I don't see how women in some times and cultures managed to stop their field work, have a baby, then strap it on their backs and keep working. I'm too pampered I suppose."

Carrie, a beautiful brunette with the most incredible lavender eyes, was Frank's wife and an attorney in town. She'd told Skye about her coming to Naconiche as a landman for her uncle's oil company to lease property for drilling. She'd pretended to be a genealogist until she could research the records and get her ducks in a row to begin leasing.

"Nothing wrong with being pampered," Mary Beth said. "I rather like it." She was sitting in a matching easy chair, ottoman under her feet. "I keep telling J.J. that I'm perfectly fine, but he hovers like an old mother hen—until John wakes up at three in the morning."

"Amazing, isn't it?" Carrie said.

Baby Lily slept in a bassinet beside Carrie's chair, and baby John slept in a matching one beside Mary Beth. Baby Elizabeth was in a playpen beside the sliding glass doors so that she could watch everything and chew on various toys. Katy and the twins played outside and in, zipping through occasionally to look at the babies. Nonie and Kelly were in the kitchen at the moment, the men were outside, drinking beer and poking things on the grill in between dips in the pool to cool off, and Belle was all over the place.

"I love your house," Skye said of the big old Victorian.

"Isn't it great?" Carried replied. "It originally belonged to Judge Outlaw, Wes's father, then to Wes and Nonie. Belle and the brothers all grew up here. Since Frank was the first one with a family, he took it over when his folks moved to the apartment over the Double Dip."

"And now there's a new generation to enjoy the place," Nonie said as she and Kelly joined them in the den.

"Are you sure I can't help?" Mary Beth said.

"Everything is done," Kelly said. "There really wasn't that much for us to do. The food is laid out on the table and the rolls are in the warming oven waiting until the guys are finished playing with the grill, which I hope is soon."

Belle stuck her head in the door. "Ready for the meat?"

"Past ready," Kelly said. "Bring it on."

Belle held open the door while Frank, Cole and J.J. trooped in, holding heaping platters of meat and corn.

Elizabeth looked at Skye, held out her arms and yelled, "Pee! Pee!"

Who could resist the little imp? Skye picked her up, and Elizabeth patted her cheeks and, with a sweet sigh, said, "Pee."

Everybody filled their plates and ate wherever they could find a place—at a table or on a TV tray or outside on the patio. J.J. cut the ice-cold watermelons, and they gorged on that as well. The kids had a seed-spitting contest, and soon the adults joined in, too. Skye didn't do too well, but it was hard to spit with a baby bouncing on your hip. Gabe won.

"It's from all that hot air you developed selling real estate," Belle said, laughing and putting her arm around his waist. "And now that we have you all gathered together, Gabe and I have an announcement to make."

"I finally wore Belle down," Gabe said. "And she's agreed to marry me." He took a box from his pocket, opened it and slipped a ring on her finger. "We're now officially engaged."

Everybody clapped and whooped, and J.J. yelled, "When's the wedding?"

"When the bluebonnets next bloom in Wimberely," Belle said.

Sam, who stood next to Skye, looked down at her as she held Elizabeth, smiled and hugged her to him. "Will that make you my sister?"

"No, I'll only be an in-law."

"Would you rather be an Outlaw?"

Skye's heart almost stopped. She didn't know what to say. Was he merely teasing?

She was saved by Elizabeth, who commanded her attention by patting Skye's cheeks and yelling, "Pee! Pit!"

"The spitting's over, sweetheart."

Kelly plucked Elizabeth from Skye's arms. "You've warted Auntie Skye too long, punkin'. Let's go find Daddy. He'll spit some more for you."

Auntie Skye? She liked the sound of it.

BACK AT THE TWILIGHT INN, Belle and Skye went to their room, opting to wait a few minutes until the coast was clear to change roommates.

"I'm going to take a quick shower," Skye said. "I'm sticky with watermelon juice."

"Don't use all the hot water," Belle said. "I want to wash off the bug spray. I think it's strange that bugs don't bite you."

"What can I say? I'm charmed."

After her shower, Skye vacated the bathroom quickly and dressed in shorts and a tank top and brushed her hair while Belle bathed. She even took time for a quick makeup repair.

Belle, too, came out in shorts and tank top. "Great minds," she said of their similar dress.

"I really like your family," Skye said.

"So do I," Belle said. "They're a rowdy bunch, but I love them, especially in small doses. They like you, too. You seem to fit right in. We'd love to have you as a permanent part of the family, more than just as Gabe's sister, I mean."

Not quite sure how to respond, Skye said, "I'm so happy about you and Gabe. When did that happen?"

"Just this week. I agreed to marry him, and he agreed to a long engagement. Besides, I love the hill country in April."

The phone rang, and Belle answered. "Give me two minutes to put on my shoes and get my toothbrush." She hung up and said, "That was Sam. The switch is on." She stepped into her flip-flops and hurried to the bathroom. When she came out, Belle said, "Turn off the porch light and peek outside to see if the coast is clear."

Skye didn't hesitate. She flipped off the outside light and cracked open the door. "Clear," she whispered.

Belle eased out the door while Skye held onto the knob, watching.

"Hold it, you scallywags! Police!" A spotlight hit Belle and Sam as they crossed between the two units.

Skye's heart leapt to her throat.

"J.J., is that you? Turn that damned light out, or I'm going to come beat you to a bloody pulp." The light died as Sam stalked toward it. "What the hell do you mean pulling a dumb stunt like that?"

Skye could hear only the rumble of low voices, one angry, one amused. Long gone, Belle had only laughed and shot into the next room. Skye was left alone, staring into the dark, when the talking stopped and Sam appeared at the door.

"I'm sorry about that, darlin'." Sam took her into his arms and kicked the door closed behind him. "My brother is a knucklehead. Are you okay?"

"I'm fine. Just startled."

"J.J. came to drop off something for the night manager, saw the lights go off and figured he'd play a joke. He didn't know how easily spooked you were. He feels lower than worm dirt and sends his sincerest apologies."

She chuckled. "Worm dirt?"

"That's close enough to what he said."

"I'm okay. I promise. I was just startled, not traumatized. And it is kind of funny. I'll bet we all looked like deer caught in headlights."

"Thanks for being a good sport about it." He kissed her gently and rubbed his cheek against hers. He'd shaved, she noticed. "I've been looking forward to doing that all day. Do you realized that we haven't had a minute alone?"

"I do."

"Come here, woman." He led her to the bed, put his pistol on the nightstand and kicked off his shoes. "I've got a powerful yen for you, but first, I have something important to tell you." He sat down on the side of the bed and pulled her into his lap.

"It sounds serious," she said, feeling a bit wary.

"Serious, but good. I finally located Dennis Mayfield's sister yesterday. She'd moved to Kilgore."

Skye's heartbeat accelerated. "And?"

"And you don't have to worry about that bastard again. He's in a North Carolina prison, sentenced to life without parole."

"What happened?"

"He pulled the same thing there. He kidnapped a college student there four years ago, but this time they caught him after he picked up the money."

"And the girl?"

"Unfortunately, she didn't make it. But he's been put away for good."

"For good?"

"Absolutely. Life without parole means just that. He'll die in prison."

Skye felt as if a heavy weight suddenly had been lifted from her, as if the thick, tight armor encasing her had shattered like glass and fallen away. She could feel her spirit soar. Throwing her arms around him, she said, "Oh, Sam, thank you. Thank you." She kissed his face over and over.

"I appreciate the thanks, darlin', but I didn't do much of anything."

"Oh, but you did. You can't know what this means to me, what you mean to me."

As if her full passion had been unleashed, she kissed him with a devouring hunger, and they made love with an intensity that left them both breathless and slick with sweat.

Afterward, they lay curled together, basking in the glow, waiting for their heartbeats to slow. "I love you so much," Sam said.

"And I love you."

A few moments later, he said, "You know, Texas Rangers don't make a lot of money."

"I'd never thought about it," she said. "Money isn't very important to me."

"I'll be a Ranger until I retire or until they kick me out. I'll never be rich, but I've never wanted to be anything but a Texas Ranger. It's who I am, who I was born to be."

"I understand. I feel that way about being a veterinarian. It's who I am."

"But your practice is in Wimberley, and my job is in San Antonio."

"So?" Skye said, rubbing her foot over his calf.

"It would be a long commute for one of us."

"I don't understand. It's a long commute now."

"I'm talking about if we got married."

Her foot stilled. "Married?"

"Yeah. And, sugar, I don't see how I could afford to employ a security force like the one you have with Gabe. I've tried and tried to figure out a way, but even with the oil lease money and the income from the wells, I don't think it would be enough to pay a bunch of salaries for bodyguards."

Skye sat straight up in bed. "Let me see if I got this straight. I'm okay to take to bed, but you're not interested in marrying me because it would be inconvenient, and I cost too much. Does that about sum it up?"

"Hell, no. I didn't mean that. I meant I'm crazy in love with you, and how in the devil are we ever going to work things out between us?"

"Did you ever think I might have some ideas about all this, or do you consider me too neurotic?" She jumped up, grabbed her shorts and top and stomped to the bathroom, locking the door behind her.

"Skye, darlin'," Sam said, knocking on the door. "We need to talk."

"We've done enough talking for now. I'm going to brush my teeth."

He kept knocking. She ignored him and took another shower.

When she finally opened the door, Sam was sitting just outside in the big green chair. He wore only his briefs, and one big foot was planted on each side of the door frame, trapping her.

"I love you, Skye. Will you marry me?"

"I'll have to think about it."

"How long will you need to think?"

"I'm not sure. We have issues."

"I've come up with an idea. I can sell the lake house and buy us a place halfway between Wimberley and San Antonio and—"

"You are *not* going to sell the lake house. I adore the lake house and so do you. That's out."

"Well, if you have a better idea, let's hear it."

"Not now. I'm tired. Let's call a truce and go to sleep. I always think better in the mornings."

WHEN SKYE WOKE UP the next morning, Belle was in the other bed. She got up and quietly made coffee. Both of them needed caffeine to function properly. She dressed, and when she came out of the bathroom, Belle was stretching.

"The coffee woke me. Smells heavenly. Thanks."

After a cup, Belle dressed, and they both packed.

"What time are we supposed to be at Kelly and Cole's house for brunch?" Skye asked.

"Ten," Belle told her. "We have plenty of time."

The guys knocked on the door and came in with their cups. Sam was eating an apple. "To keep up my strength until brunch," he said. "Y'all want to go look at where they're drilling the oil wells? Carrie says they expect to hit any day now."

They packed the car, turned in their keys and made a detour by the drilling site before they arrived at Cole and Kelly's house. They were met with hugs, and a lovely scent of cinnamon permeated the air.

"Something smells good," Sam said.

"You always think about your stomach," Skye said. "Kelly, your house is darling. I just love it."

"Come on, and I'll give you the nickle tour. Cole, pour these people some coffee and juice. We'll be right there."

Kelly showed Skye around the three bedrooms and the den that overlooked a patio with an old-fashioned swing.

"I see you have a garage apartment," Skye said as she peered out the bay window.

"The housekeeper and my cats live there."

"Your cats?"

"Cole's allergic. We're going to get a puppy when Elizabeth is a little older."

Skye smiled. "I know just what I'm giving her for her birthday. Maybe even sooner. I have some adorable half-poodle puppies that will need homes."

After brunch, they got on the road home, Belle and Gabe in his car, Skye and Sam in his.

"You know," Skye said after they'd gone about twenty miles through the forested landscape, "I'd been thinking about my living arrangements since things began to look serious between Gabe and Belle. I adore Belle, but I don't think it's right for three women to share a roof. Mom and I have discussed it, too. She's considering taking over Belle's townhouse."

"What about Tiger? I thought they didn't allow pets there."

Skye smiled. "You don't know my mother. It won't be a problem."

"And what about you?"

"You know, I've been thinking about moving my practice and buying my own place. I've done fairly well over the years, and my expenses aren't all that much. Gabe has invested for me in both real estate and equities. I've got money of my own to finance my needs."

"Where are you planning to move your practice?"

"I thought San Antonio might be good. My former roommate Lisa is there, you know. Did I mention that she's a veterinarian, too? She'd love to have me join her practice. What do you think of that idea?"

Sam grinned. "I think it's a fine idea. When did you plan to do that?"

"I thought maybe in the spring. That will give me time to find a house and finish up with my therapy."

"Want to move into my townhouse with me?"

"I'd like to have something bigger, maybe something big enough for horses and for Carlotta and the sheep. And maybe a small house for Maria and Manuel."

"Darlin', I can't afford all that."

"I haven't asked you to. I'm just talking about my plans. Did you know that Kelly had her own house and a house-keeper when she and Cole married? Think about your sisters-in-law. Carrie is an attorney. Mary Beth owns a tearoom and a motel. Even your mother, who taught school for so long, still works running the shop. They all earn money and share living expenses with their spouses. It seems reasonable to me.

"I'm a veterinarian. I'm good at what I do, and I earn a fair amount of money doing it. Plus, I love it. Between the two of us, we can live quite comfortably. What do you think?"

Sam didn't say anything right away, and she began to grow fidgety. He pulled over in a rest stop and turned off the engine. He unbuckled his seat belt, then hers, and pulled her close. "I get it," he said. "It's a great idea. But how are you going to feel about leaving Wimberley, about leaving the security of the compound?"

"I feel that's it's a new beginning. A little scary but very exciting. I'll probably never be able to go caving with you— or maybe I will—but I think most of my fears are behind me. Something profound happened to me when you told me that Dennis was in prison. The grip on my heart loosened. I feel free, really free. Oh, I'll take normal safety precautions, but I won't need a bodyguard. Except Gus. I'll always have Gus."

"Will you marry me, Skye Walker?"

"Yes," she said, wrapping her arms around his neck. "Yes, I will. In the spring when the bluebonnets bloom."

She kissed him with all the love in her heart, knowing that he was her knight in shining armor, sent just for her.

A golden-cheeked warbler landed on the hood of the car and sang while they made their promises to each other.

Epilogue

Two days before the wedding, Skye and Sam stood in the bedroom of their new home in San Antonio. It was on twenty acres that had a small creek running through the property. The three-bedroom house on the land had needed only a little updating, and the place also featured a practically new barn and a darling two bedroom house, ideal for Maria and Manuel, who were delighted to move nearer their oldest daughter. The furniture had been delivered earlier in the week.

"Can you believe how we lucked out?" Skye asked. "Everything fits the house perfectly. And the price was right, too."

"You can't get much better than free," Sam said. "Good thing for us that Belle insisted on getting rid of all Gabe's furniture."

"Who can blame her? Can you imagine living in a house decorated by your husband's former fiancé? And, you know, the stuff looks totally different in this house. It doesn't bother me that it's secondhand. Does it bother you?"

"Nope. If you're happy, I'm happy. When are we going to move the animals down here?"

"I thought after we got back from our honeymoon."

"Good idea."

Everything was ready for them to move in—except for putting up one last painting. Skye wanted to hang it across from their bed so that she could see it every morning and remember how blessed she was. It had been a wedding gift from her mother.

Sam's soul painting.

It was a large canvas in a silver leaf frame. Sam was depicted dressed in silver armor on a big white horse. Instead of a helmet, he wore a white-ten gallon hat, and he was smiling with an inner radiance that took her breath away. He had a long lance in one hand and a gun was strapped to his opposite hip. His Texas Ranger badge glittered on his chest, and a wispy blue scarf fluttered from where it was tied to his arm. A cherubic Pookie, complete with tiny angel wings, hovered over his left shoulder.

"I wish I knew what those symbols along the side and bottom meant," he said. "I don't have a clue."

"Mom always adds something that will make sense in time. She's captured you exactly. You're a modern-day knight."

"I don't know about that, but I know that looking at this painting makes me feel good."

Skye marked the spot, and Sam hammered the hanger onto their freshly painted wall. The wall was pale yellow, the color of soft morning sunshine.

He hung the painting. "Is that straight?"

"It's perfect. Everything is perfect."

He gave her a quick kiss. "I've got to get back to the office and get work done, and you need to get on the road."

"I know."

They walked out together, and Gus met them in the front hall, where he had waited. He and Sam had gotten to be better friends in the past few months, and he no longer growled when Sam kissed her. Thank heaven for little miracles.

Sam set the alarm and locked the door behind them while she got out her car keys. She drove everywhere now, no problem. And she had concluded her sessions with Barbara Gossett before Christmas.

Skye was glad that she and Sam had waited until now to get married. She'd needed the time to prepare. Now she was ready. The awful thing from her past that had crippled her for so long had been conquered. She could live again.

She patted the limestone wall beside the door. "Bye, house. We'll see you in a few days."

Arm in arm, they walked down the winding stone pathway, through the gate on to their cars, Gus following.

Sam held open her door and saw that she was safely buckled in, then stuck his head through the window and kissed her. Gus only panted quietly from the backseat. "I'll see you Saturday, darlin'—unless you change your mind."

"I'm not changing my mind. Call me tonight."

"Don't I always?"

He stood by his car and waved as she drove away. She honked the horn and waved back.

Skye drove by her new office on her way out of town. Her name was already on the sign, but she wouldn't start work there for two weeks. Happily, Napoleon had agreed to join her and continue as her assistant. Things wouldn't have been the same without Napoleon.

Checking the time, she speeded up to get back to Wimberley. Even though they were having a small double wedding with Belle and Gabe, there were a million last-minute things to do, and the Outlaw clan were hitting town tomorrow. They were all coming. Wes and Nonie would stay at the house, and Gabe had rented an entire guest ranch for the others.

She was eager to see the family and hear how the puppies were doing. She had given the apricot one to Elizabeth and the black ones to Katy and the twins. Funny, she'd planned to keep Nana, who had become part of the family, but as soon as the puppies were gone, Nana had left and had never come back.

Skye liked to think that she'd found another orphaned litter who needed her.

Bluebonnets, dotted here and there with patches of Indian paintbrush, bloomed in profusion along the roadside. The wildflowers seemed especially beautiful this spring. Belle said that they wouldn't have dared not to. She was counting on them for the wedding.

When she arrived home, Skye got a banana from the kitchen and walked out to the pasture where Carlotta, the llama, tended her two sheep charges. She climbed up on the fence and Carlotta came running to greet her. Drawn by the banana, she was sure. The llama adored bananas.

Pinching off a piece, she handed it to Carlotta, who nibbled it lustily.

Skye stroked her head. "We'll be moving to a new place soon. I think you'll like it."

Carlotta looked at her with big llama eyes and seemed to smile.

GABE HAD GONE ALL OUT, Sam thought as he stood by the altar with his friend and faced the small group of family and close friends that sat in the rows of white chairs. A large white tent had been pitched in a huge field of bluebonnets that Gabe said was on property he'd given Belle as a wedding gift. The gentle roll of the land was a carpet of blue. He'd never seen anything quite so awesome.

Until he looked up and saw his bride coming down the aisle on Ralph's arm. She made his heart skip. She looked like a fairy princess in her white gown and veil. Belle and her father walked beside them, but he couldn't pay much attention to his sister for watching Skye. She seemed to float. His chest swelled with pride—and with love, swelled so big that he couldn't catch his breath.

The next thing he knew Skye and Belle were standing there and the minister said, "Dearly beloved, we are gathered here…"

And he was the happiest man in the universe.

* * * * *

Mediterranean Nights

Join the guests and crew of Alexandra's Dream, *the newest luxury ship to set sail on the romantic Mediterranean, as they experience the glamorous world of cruising.*

A new Harlequin continuity series begins in June 2007 with FROM RUSSIA, WITH LOVE by Ingrid Weaver

Marina Artamova books a cabin on the luxurious cruise ship Alexandra's Dream, *when she finds out that her orphaned nephew and his adoptive father are aboard. She's determined to be reunited with the boy... but the romantic ambience of the ship and her undeniable attraction to a man she considers her enemy are about to interfere with her quest!*

Turn the page for a sneak preview!

Piraeus, Greece

"THERE SHE IS, Stefan. *Alexandra's Dream*." David Anderson squatted beside his new son and pointed at the dark blue hull that towered above the pier. The cruise ship was a majestic sight, twelve decks high and as long as a city block. A circle of silver and gold stars, the logo of the Liberty Cruise Line, gleamed from the swept-back smokestack. Like some legendary sea creature born for the water, the ship emanated power from every sleek curve—even at rest it held the promise of motion. "That's going to be our home for the next ten days."

The child beside him remained silent, his cheeks working in and out as he sucked furiously on his thumb. Hair so blond it appeared white ruffled against his forehead in the harbor breeze. The baby-sweet scent unique to the very young mingled with the tang of the sea.

"Ship," David said. "Uh, *parakhod*."

From beneath his bangs, Stefan looked at the *Alexandra's Dream*. Although he didn't release his thumb, the corners of his mouth tightened with the beginning of a smile.

David grinned. That was Stefan's first smile this afternoon, one of only two since they had left the orphanage yesterday. It was probably because of the boat—according to the orphanage staff, the boy loved boats, which was the main reason David had decided to book this cruise. Then again, there was a strong possibility the smile could have been a reaction to David's attempt at pocket-dictionary Russian. Whatever the cause, it was a good start.

The liaison from the adoption agency had claimed that Stefan had been taught some English, but David had yet to see evidence of it. David continued to speak, positive his son would understand his tone even if he couldn't grasp the words. "This is her maiden voyage. Her first trip, just like this is our first trip, and that makes it special." He motioned toward the stage that had been set up on the pier beneath the ship's bow. "That's why everyone's celebrating."

The ship's official christening ceremony had been held the day before and had been a closed affair, with only the cruise-line executives and VIP guests invited, but the stage hadn't yet been disassembled. Banners bearing the blue and white of the Greek flag of the ship's owner, as well as the Liberty circle of stars logo, draped the edges of the platform. In the center, a group of musicians and a dance troupe dressed in traditional white folk costumes performed for the benefit of the *Alexandra's Dream*'s first passengers. Their audience was in a festive mood, snapping their fingers in time to the music while the dancers twirled and wove through their steps.

David bobbed his head to the rhythm of the mandolins. They were playing a folk tune that seemed vaguely familiar, possibly from a movie he'd seen. He hummed a few notes. "Catchy melody, isn't it?"

Stefan turned his gaze on David. His eyes were a striking shade of blue, as cool and pale as a winter horizon and far too solemn for a child not yet five. Still, the smile that hovered at the corners of his mouth persisted. He moved his head with the music, mirroring David's motion.

David gave a silent cheer at the interaction. Hopefully, this cruise would provide countless opportunities for more. "Hey, good for you," he said. "Do you like the music?"

The child's eyes sparked. He withdrew his thumb with a pop. *"Moozika!"*

"Music. Right!" David held out his hand. "Come on, let's go closer so we can watch the dancers."

Stefan grasped David's hand quickly, as if he feared it would be withdrawn. In an instant his budding smile was replaced by a look close to panic.

Did he remember the car accident that had killed his parents? It would be a mercy if he didn't. As far as David knew, Stefan had never spoken of it to anyone. Whatever he had seen had made him run so far from the crash that the police hadn't found him until the next day. The event had traumatized him to the extent that he hadn't uttered a word until his fifth week at the orphanage. Even now he seldom talked.

David sat back on his heels and brushed the hair from Stefan's forehead. That solemn, too-old gaze locked with his, and for an instant, David felt as if he looked back in time at an image of himself thirty years ago.

He didn't need to speak the same language to understand exactly how this boy felt. He knew what it meant to be alone and powerless among strangers, trying to be brave and tough but wishing with every fiber of his being for a place to belong, to be safe, and most of all for someone to love him….

He knew in his heart he would be a good parent to Stefan. It was why he had never considered halting the adoption process after Ellie had left him. He hadn't balked when he'd learned of the recent claim by Stefan's spinster aunt, either; the absentee relative had shown up too late for her case to be considered. The adoption was meant to be. He and this child already shared a bond that went deeper than paperwork or legalities.

A seagull screeched overhead, making Stefan start and press closer to David.

"That's my boy," David murmured. He swallowed hard, struck by the simple truth of what he had just said.

That's my *boy*.

"I CAN'T BE PATIENT, RUDOLPH. I'm not going to stand by and watch my nephew get ripped from his country and his roots to live on the other side of the world."

Rudolph hissed out a slow breath. "Marina, I don't like the sound of that. What are you planning?"

"I'm going to talk some sense into this American kidnapper."

"No. Absolutely not. No offence, but diplomacy is not your strong suit."

"Diplomacy be damned. Their ship's due to sail at five o'clock."

"Then you wouldn't have an opportunity to speak with him even if his lawyer agreed to a meeting."

"I'll have ten days of opportunities, Rudolph, since I plan to be on board that ship."

* * * * *

*Follow Marina and David as they join forces to uncover
the reason behind little Stefan's unusual silence,
and the secret behind the death of his parents....*

Look for From Russia, With Love
*by Ingrid Weaver
in stores June 2007.*

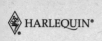

Mediterranean NIGHTS™

Tycoon Elias Stamos is launching his newest luxury cruise ship from his home port in Greece. But someone from his past is eager to expose old secrets and to see the Stamos empire crumble.

Mediterranean Nights
launches in June 2007 with...

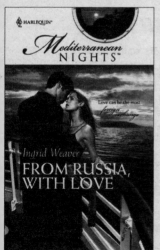

FROM RUSSIA, WITH LOVE
by *Ingrid Weaver*

Join the guests and crew of *Alexandra's Dream* as they are drawn into a world of glamour, romance and intrigue in this new 12-book series.

www.eHarlequin.com

MN1

REQUEST YOUR FREE BOOKS!
2 FREE NOVELS PLUS 2
FREE GIFTS!

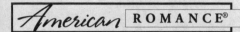 **ROMANCE®**

Heart, Home & Happiness!

YES! Please send me 2 FREE Harlequin American Romance® novels and my 2 FREE gifts. After receiving them, if I don't wish to receive any more books, I can return the shipping statement marked "cancel." If I don't cancel, I will receive 4 brand-new novels every month and be billed just $4.24 per book in the U.S., or $4.99 per book in Canada, plus 25¢ shipping and handling per book and applicable taxes, if any*. That's a savings of close to 15% off the cover price! I understand that accepting the 2 free books and gifts places me under no obligation to buy anything. I can always return a shipment and cancel at any time. Even if I never buy another book from Harlequin, the two free books and gifts are mine to keep forever.   154 HDN EEZK   354 HDN EEZV

Name _____ (PLEASE PRINT) _____

Address _____ Apt. # _____

City _____ State/Prov. _____ Zip/Postal Code _____

Signature (if under 18, a parent or guardian must sign)

Mail to the **Harlequin Reader Service®:**
IN U.S.A.: P.O. Box 1867, Buffalo, NY 14240-1867
IN CANADA: P.O. Box 609, Fort Erie, Ontario L2A 5X3

Not valid to current Harlequin American Romance subscribers.

Want to try two free books from another line?
Call 1-800-873-8635 or visit www.morefreebooks.com.

* Terms and prices subject to change without notice. NY residents add applicable sales tax. Canadian residents will be charged applicable provincial taxes and GST. This offer is limited to one order per household. All orders subject to approval. Credit or debit balances in a customer's account(s) may be offset by any other outstanding balance owed by or to the customer. Please allow 4 to 6 weeks for delivery.

Your Privacy: Harlequin is committed to protecting your privacy. Our Privacy Policy is available online at www.eHarlequin.com or upon request from the Reader Service. From time to time we make our lists of customers available to reputable firms who may have a product or service of interest to you. If you would prefer we not share your name and address, please check here. ☐

HAR07

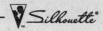

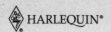
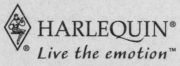

667.50

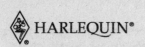
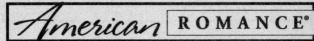
COMING NEXT MONTH

#1165 SUMMER LOVIN' by Marin Thomas, Laura Marie Altom and Ann Roth

This year, celebrating the Fourth of July in Silver Cliff, Colorado, is going to be special. There's an all-year high school reunion taking place before the school building gets torn down. As old flames find each other and new romances begin, this season this small town is looking like the perfect place for some summer lovin'!

#1166 THE COWGIRL'S CEO by Pamela Britton

Barrel-racing star Caroline Sheppard wants only one thing: to win the NFR, the Super Bowl of rodeos. But she can't get there without help from millionaire businessman Tyler Harrison. And his sponsorship comes with strings attached. But even if Caro wants to turn him down, her heart, as Ty is about to learn, is as big as the Wyoming sky....

#1167 THE MAN FOR MAGGIE by Lee McKenzie

Having distanced himself from his wealthy family, Nick Durrance started his own construction business, and now pretty much keeps to himself. But Maggie Meadowcroft sees something special in the man and decides to work some magic on him to see if she can't reconnect him with his family and friends. But when he starts falling for Maggie, things get really interesting!

#1168 HIS ONLY WIFE by Cathy McDavid

Aubrey Stuart is reluctant to get involved with hotshot firefighter Gage Raintree. She loved him once, but now her life and her job as a nurse is in Tucson, far away from the small town of Blue Ridge. At the end of the summer she will have to leave—is the persistent Gage going to let her?

HARCNM0507